Darke
A Thornton Brothers Time Travel Romance Novel
Book 1

Cynthia Luhrs

This book is a work of fiction. Names, characters, places, and incidents either are products of the author's imagination or are used fictitiously.

Darkest Knight, A Thornton Brothers Time Travel Romance Novel

Copyright © 2016 by Cynthia Luhrs

Acknowledgments

Thanks to my fabulous editor, Arran at Editing720
and Kendra at Typos Be Gone.

May each and every one of you find your very own
knight in shining armor.

Chapter One

Prologue

Melinda held Emma Pittypat Rivers on her lap. The door opened and a messenger staggered in. James took the message and called for the healer. Two of his knights took the man to the kitchen. James read the missive, his face turning a grayish color. Alarm spread through her.

"Call William and Henry in from the lists."

Melinda took Emma and put the sleeping baby in a cradle so she wouldn't wake and start crying. "What's happened?"

"I must speak with Henry."

"I am here," Henry said as he strode into the room, the rest following behind him.

James looked grim. "You should sit."

Melinda looked at him, and some kind of unspoken message seemed to pass between them. She was glad both her sisters were spending the summer at Falconburg.

"I swore I would never breathe a word. He didn't want you to go around stirring up trouble."

Henry looked confused. "What the bloody hell are you on about?"

"'Tis your brother. John."

"John is dead."

James shook his head. "Nay. He is alive. John is the infamous bandit in the woods. He has been betrayed. Your brother is imprisoned in the tower, awaiting death."

Chapter Two

Present day—London, England

Anna caught a glimpse of the jewels through the crowds. The moving walkway slowly inched closer, bringing her within drooling distance of the jewels safely protected behind glass. Not paying attention, she tripped, heard a few nasty remarks, and found herself jostled back at least twenty feet. Her toe throbbed where the tall woman in front of her had stepped hard on her foot. The black canvas shoes were comfortable for walking around the city but certainly not made to protect your toes from grouchy tourists.

A large tour group pushed and shoved, and the next thing Anna knew she was at the exit. Some days being petite totally stunk.

A hand on her arm startled her. "Miss. Step aside."

Before Anna could protest, the guard winked at her. He leaned close. "Stand here a moment, miss."

With a deep, booming voice that reminded her of a bell, the guard called out, "The tower is closing. Walk on."

While she waited for everyone to finish going by the jewels, Anna rubbed her ankle. It was chilly in the room and she took a moment to zip up the hoodie she'd brought with her. A t-shirt wasn't going to cut it. She swore the woman in front of her, who looked rather like a giant possum, purposely stepped on Anna's foot with her stiletto heels. Who wore heels to sightsee?

Her foot throbbed. *Guess that's what you get for wearing comfortable shoes to walk around London.*

The last of the crowds filed out, the woman snootily looking Anna up and down as she exited the room. The guard's light blue eyes twinkled beneath his hat as he smiled down kindly at her.

"You remind me of my granddaughter. Lives across the pond. Married an actor." He scratched his ear. "I've seen his films," he said. "They're all rubbish, if you ask me."

Unable to hold it in, Anna giggled. "It sure gets crowded in here."

"Aye. It's almost closing time, miss. I can give you ten minutes to take a closer look." He motioned to the jewels winking in the light.

Grateful for his kindness, she moved closer. The dark backdrop showed off the jewels to perfection. What would it be like to hold the stones in her hand? Other than the guard, she had the room to herself. Anna swore she could feel the history in the room permeating the walls. Kings and queens over the centuries looking down from above.

What must they think of the people gawking at their jewels? Likely the same as when they were in power. People then probably gaped and gawked to get a closer look at royalty and their belongings just as they did today.

It only seemed like a few minutes had passed when the guard cleared his throat. "It's time to close up. I've let you stay rather longer than I should have." He pointed to the left. "Go through the door; you'll see signs directing you to the exit. Stay on the path. Odd things have been known to happen on the grounds after hours."

Barely resisting the urge to hug him, Anna shook his hand instead. "You've been very kind to me. Thank you. It must be wonderful to come here every day to work."

The guard, who reminded her of a kind grandfather, ducked his head. "One certainly sees interesting folks come through." He looked at his watch. "Hurry along now. Don't want either of us to get in trouble."

Walking at a brisk pace down the corridor, Anna looked for the exit signs. The sound of the steel shutters reverberated down the empty hallway. Her phone told her it was a quarter after four. Fifteen minutes until everything would be locked up tight for the night. The wind rushing over the stone sounded a bit like a moan.

Anna picked up the pace, the rubber soles of her shoes quiet against the stone. Where was everybody? The workers must be pretty efficient to get everyone out so quickly. She seemed to be the only tourist left.

The signs led her outside. Where were the guards? Maybe they were locking up. She better be quick. Following the walk, she turned right to make her way back to the street exit. As she passed the White Tower, Anna hunched her shoulders. The guide said it was built to strike fear into the hearts of mere mortals. It certainly worked on her. She couldn't imagine what it would be like to be imprisoned here.

Another quick glance at her watch told her she had a few precious minutes left. When she came in, Anna missed the raven's graveyard. If she didn't see them now, she never would. Tomorrow she planned to visit Stonehenge. Surely she would have time to take a super-fast look.

The guide said there were seven ravens in residence at the tower, the required six and one to spare. She'd always been fascinated by the big blackbirds. Though she thought what they ate was a little bit disgusting. Biscuits and blood. Gross. The man said the birds ate raw meat every day, plus the bird biscuits soaked in blood. So not a job she'd want. No way would she ever complain about picking up dirty dishes after customers left the diner.

Black feathers caught her eye and she squinted to make out the marker the raven sat atop. The bird seemed to be saying, *Aren't I fabulous?* Raindrops spattered the screen of her phone as she snapped a picture to post. The dark clouds overhead made her hurry.

Somehow she must've turned left when she should have turned right, because now Anna found herself far from the main exit. It was plenty warm outside, but with the rain she started to feel chilly. Where was a guard or guide when you needed them? Thunder cracked overhead and Anna looked for a place to shelter until the rain stopped. Great, just great. Ever since she was little, Anna hated thunderstorms. Surely they wouldn't mind if she waited a few more minutes?

The plaque informed her she was in the Bloody Tower. The next boom made her jump. The air smelled like wet stone and something electrical burning. She hunched her shoulders and leaned back against the wall inside the doorway, trying to make herself small.

Something clicked. Anna fell backward into darkness.

"Ouch."

She landed awkwardly on her sore ankle. With her thumb she slid the phone on to use it as a flashlight. A rat scurried by, making her shriek. There was the faint outline of a door. With a finger, she traced the lines of cold stone, looking for a way to open the secret door.

No matter what she did, it wouldn't open. Anna screamed and pounded on the stone but no one came. They probably couldn't hear her behind the stone walls, especially with the storm raging outside. While Anna hoped the history of the tower would seep into her pores, this wasn't exactly what she had in mind.

The bright light of the phone showed her a set of stairs. Up or down? No way up would lead outside. Down, then. The narrow steps curved to the right. Good —if she kept to the right she out to come out near the gates. Fingers crossed.

The stairs ended in a small room with two doors and an open corridor. Neither door would budge. She kept walking down the hallway, looking for a way out. It seemed like she'd been here an awful long time. At first Anna thought maybe the guards used the passages to travel between the buildings. But when she shined the light on the floor, it looked like the dust hadn't been disturbed in ages. Cobwebs brushed her hair and she saw two more rats while she made her way through the stone passageways.

The only good thing about rats was that if they were here they must know a way out, right?

Boy oh boy, wouldn't Hattie laugh when she heard about this. Her poor friend. Jilted at the altar. Anna remembered standing there, in the bright lemon dress, watching her friend crumple. It had been awful. She despised Ben for what he had done, yet if he hadn't jilted her best friend, Anna wouldn't be here. How could you be angry and happy at the same time?

A week after the failed wedding, Hattie had popped over for a glass of sweet tea. As they lounged by the pool on one of Anna's extremely rare days off, her friend slid an envelope across the table. Hattie had cashed in both tickets for one business-class ticket to London and insisted she go. Hattie was moving back to Indiana to be close to her family and would never think of England again without thinking of Ben. It had been their dream vacation. Anna would miss her terribly.

When Anna arrived in England, she swore the very air was filled with history and possibility. Who could have dreamed she'd be locked in the infamous Tower of London after hours?

Another door loomed in front of her. She tried it, and wasn't sure if it was her imagination, but the door seemed to move slightly. With everything she had, which wasn't much, given she was only five foot four, Anna leaned against it with her shoulder and pushed with every ounce of strength she had.

No luck. "Oh, come on. This is what you get for eating pancakes for breakfast instead of a healthy green smoothie."

With a deep breath, she leaned back and shoved the

door again. It gave way and she went sprawling onto the floor. She started to shiver but resisted the urge to look over her shoulder. Whatever room she was in, the air felt full of menace and anger.

It was almost six. The tower was closed and no one had found her. The room she found herself in was dusty and full of cobwebs. Not a single footprint to be found in the thin layer of dirt on the stone floor. Obviously there weren't any cameras either. Otherwise someone would have come and found her and scolded her as they escorted her out. Or more likely had her arrested.

"I can't be stuck here until morning. It's beyond creepy." Anna shined the light of her dying phone around the room again. "If there's an axe murderer hiding in here or a ghost intent on killing me, I haven't done very much yet with my life, so how about a pass?"

It was silly talking to the darkness, but it made her feel better. At least wherever she was the stone muffled the sound of the storm. As she was thinking happy thoughts, a moan made the hair all over her body stand on end. "Please tell me that was the wind."

Anna felt a breeze coming from the stone near her head. As she ran her hands over the wall, something clicked and she fell through another passageway.

Chapter Three

England—July 1331

"There is trouble afoot. We cannot go north now that the Scots are allied with the French. Who knows how long this war will be. 'Tis long overdue for us to find a new home. Make everyone ready to travel in a fortnight."

"Too many are ill. They cannot travel now. Once they heal we will go south. Be wary. There is an ill wind tonight, John."

He spoke sharply: "Do not call me by name. That name died with the man a long, long time ago."

The healer pursed her lips and pointed to two men running as fast as their legs could carry them.

"A fat noble in a richly appointed carriage is

trespassing through the wood. We could use the horses." The man leaned over, hands on his knees, sucking in deep gulps of air.

The other man hopped from foot to foot. "I smell a large purse of gold. Perhaps jewels and furs. Shall we take him?"

John's mood lifted. A prize was exactly what he needed. Thinking of war made him irritable.

"Lead on."

A small band of men made their way through the wood, silent as the creatures that shared their home.

"My lord. 'Tis not wise to enter the dark wood. Many who do are never seen again."

The noble made a rude gesture. "I am in a hurry to see my mistress. The path through the wood is the fastest route. Move on."

The carriage jolted forward, the horses jerking on the reins. The animals smelled John and his men hiding in the brush. With a wave of his hand, chaos ensued.

"What have we here? A fat noble trespassing through my wood." John pushed off the tree and sauntered up to eye his prize.

The man looked nervous, sweating and wiping his brow. "How dare you stop me? Let me pass."

John didn't bother to answer. Instead he nodded to the men, who made quick work of unhitching the horses.

"You should have listened to your driver. Fortune is

with you this day. I am in a magnanimous mood and will let you live." John eyed the man's plump hands, the jewels sparkling in the sunlight. An ornate ring adorning every sausage-shaped finger. "I will take the jewels. Every single one."

The noble spluttered and swore as he removed the jewels. As he handed them over he sneered at John. "The king will hear of this treachery."

"Don't forget the chest." John inclined his head. "I care not what you tell the king." He pulled the man from the carriage, tossing him to the ground.

"Let them go. Keep the belongings. The horses we will make use of. Sell the carriage."

He turned to the red-faced noble. The fool carried not a single blade upon his person. How could he be so arrogant?

"Go now and I will let you live."

The man opened his mouth then shut it with a snap. He trudged out of the wood muttering, the driver following behind.

Back at the camp, the men were in good spirits. 'Twas a good catch. A fat purse, a large trunk containing jewels and gold and many furs. John could feed his people and provide all they would need.

"Archie. You'll easily sell the carriage at the Boar's Head Inn. Take three men with you to bring the horses back. I will meet you there later this eve."

"Is that wise? The bounty on your head has been

raised yet again."

"Let them raise it. I will not live my life in fear of other men."

The boy stood inside the door of John's hut. "A message from Archie."

John opened the missive and squinted to read the handwriting. Archie was barely literate, and he had a hard time making out the words. "Bloody hell."

Magda appeared as he was striding across the clearing.

"Do not go out this night. Send one of the others."

"I cannot. You know we have many sick with fever." He patted her arm. "I trust you above all others to lead them to safety if anything should happen. We have discussed this many times. You know what needs be done."

She threw up her hands. "I will not argue with you. It would be wiser to talk to one of the horses." Her voice softened. "Promise you will take care."

Minutes later he was riding for the inn. By now he knew every path through the wood. Moonlight shone down, turning the night to day. From a distance, he could see light from the windows. Riding into the courtyard, he called for the stable boy. John dismounted and tossed the reins to the sleepy boy. "I shall not be long."

Entering the smoky building, he let his eyes adjust to the dimness. Archie relaxed in a corner with a well-dressed traveler. Not a noble, not a soldier, perhaps a rich merchant. John made his way through the crowd to the men. On his way, a tavern wench stopped him.

"Haven't seen you in a while."

"Not tonight, love."

She pouted and sauntered away. John faced the men.

"Archie. You should be abed."

His man was pale and sweating. Perhaps he was sicker than John realized. As Archie pushed back from the table, the man next to him placed a hand on his arm. John narrowed his eyes. Something was amiss. Once more, he looked around the room. Small details he'd missed in his haste to check on Archie fell into place. He noted the furtive looks, hands within cloaks. Cloaks in the middle of July. Inside the stifling room. His back to the wall, John frowned.

"Why?"

The man beside Archie threw off his cloak, as did others in the inn. The bloody king's men.

"I took you in when you had nothing. Gave you a home. Family."

The man tossed a bag of gold on the table. "For your

service, Archie."

"Gold? You betrayed me for a bag of gold?"

This man had lived with John for the past three years. He dropped his head, unable to meet John's eyes.

He snarled at the traitor. "You are a coward. Mark my words. You will die for your betrayal."

The well-to-do man beside him scoffed. "You're in no position to be making threats, John Thornton."

John's head snapped up.

The man sneered. "Yes. We know who you are. Archie here listened very closely to a conversation you shared with Lord Falconburg over a year ago."

The betrayal cut deeply. John didn't bother to respond. He was too busy thinking of his brothers, and of Lord Falconburg and his wife. Because of who he had become, they were all in danger.

"You're coming with us."

John didn't bother to ask where. For he knew. The tower. There were too many for him to resist. The king's men shoved him into a barred cage set atop a wagon.

"Might I have the pleasure of your name?" John looked down on the well-dressed man.

"Don't you recognize me?" The man stepped closer. He spat at John. "Whoreson. I am Lord Denby. Letitia's husband. You shamed me across all of England."

"Letitia came to me of her own free will. I did not shame you. You shamed yourself by whoring your wife to the king."

Lord Denby's fist connected with John's nose, snapping his head back. Blood poured down his face. John spat the blood into the straw and laughed, as Denby cradled his fist, howling in pain.

"Our sire found favor with another so Letitia told the king about me to make him jealous. All of this was your wife's doing."

Then, before Denby could strike him again, John reached through the bars and pulled the man close. "You are a fool."

He released Denby and stepped back. The short man did not notice John now held his dagger. He took aim and let loose. The blade found its mark in Archie's throat and his betrayer went down with a gurgle. In time he would find a way to repay Denby as well.

"No one betrays the bandit of the wood and lives to tell the tale."

Chapter Four

"Seriously! This is getting ridiculous."

Anna stood, brushing the dust off her jeans. Another room. From the looks of it, this section of the tower had been used to house prisoners. So therefore there must be an exit, right?

There were six cells in the room. She went in, checked for another hidden door and moved on to the next. The last cell on the right had a small window. Perhaps she could figure out where she was. Anna pushed up on tiptoe, and her forehead reached the bottom of the window ledge.

"You've got to be kidding me." Normally her lack of height didn't bother her, but today it was proving to be a complete pain in the behind. She jumped, straining to see out, but only caught glimpses of a dark gray sky, fifty shades of storm. Lightning arced across the sky and she stepped back, swallowing hard. A gleam in the corner of the cell caught her eye.

The light on the phone illuminated the object. She bent down and picked it up, wiping the grime off on her jeans. They were dark blue so it shouldn't show, and by this point she was already covered in dust and spider webs.

It was a locket. She turned the piece over in her hand; it felt heavy. She pried it open to see one side was empty and the other side contained an image. The grime rubbed away, she could make out a portrait. Or rather half a portrait of a man. He wore a black shirt over a muscular torso. If only she could see the face. Over and over, she ran her thumb over the ragged edge of the portrait where the top piece of the miniature had been ripped away.

She turned it over and rubbed the back. There was some type of inscription. Holding it close to the light, she tried to make it out, but it was mostly worn away. There seemed to be a word. She squinted, pushed the button on her phone, and groaned. No more battery. There might be enough light coming in from the window. Mesmerized by the locket, she tripped over an uneven section of the floor and went down hard on her knees, skinning her palms on the rough stone.

"Ouch." There was blood on her hand and on the locket. Would it ruin what was left of the artwork? A loud ringing noise filled her head, and Anna pressed her palms over her ears, heedless of the blood. It sounded like she was in the middle of the storm. Thunder boomed around her and lightning flashed inside the small cell. Which should have been impossible, given she was inside the stone walls. But blue light arced all around her.

The noise reached a crescendo and Anna wrapped her arms around herself, rocking back and forth in the corner, wishing it would stop. She closed her eyes tight and repeated over and over, "Please make it go away, please make it go away, please make it go away."

It rained the entire bloody way to London. For a full fortnight. John swore he felt every rut in the path along the way. Several days into the journey, he managed to dispatch one of the guards and almost escape before he was clouted on the back of the head and fell unconscious.

When he woke, he found himself chained in the cage.

"Won't be making the same mistake again," the guard sneered.

After that, the men were much more wary around

him. Truth be told, John was rather vexed. Had his reputation not preceded him? These men should be shaking in their boots to have captured the infamous bandit of the wood.

Movement woke him. The horses, sensing home, had picked up the pace. He rubbed his eyes. There in the distance stood the tower, the stone harsh against the clear blue sky. Given his circumstances, John thought it would have been more appropriate for it to be raining and thundering, with great clouds set against the forbidding structure, but instead it was a day to be outside enjoying life.

He was roughly hauled out of the cage, and John's knees buckled. The cage hadn't been tall enough for him to stand up straight.

"Get up with ye," one of the guards snarled.

There were two guards in front of him, one on either side, and two behind him. This was more like it. He deserved to make his entrance in style.

"Bloody hell, the stench in could here fell a horse."

"Aren't we proud, *my lord.*"

Two of the guards snickered. As unbearable as the stench was, it was the screams and moaning of broken men that made him feel the first shiver of unease. Most highborn prisoners were provided decent cells. But John Thornton hadn't been Lord Blackmoor in a very long time. And it seemed he wouldn't be Lord Blackmoor again, if the new king had his way. Why did the king care what he had done? It wasn't his mistress John had been caught with.

As they dragged him into the dark, dank bowels of the tower, he wondered if Blackmoor Castle still stood. Were any of his men still there, waiting? Mayhap one of his brothers had taken over his home. Pushing the vexing thoughts aside, John peered into the cells as they led him through the corridors.

If he were still considered high rank, he would be beheaded. As the bandit of the wood, likely he would be hanged, drawn, and quartered. He spent a moment surveying his chances of a quick death.

The constable of the tower stood waiting beside the entrance to the cell. The man held John's pouch in his hand. The tingle of coins could be heard as he threw the pouch up in the air and caught it.

"This will likely do for a while. 'Tis ten pounds for the pleasure of staying here. The rest will cover your food and accommodations."

"Who's the bandit now?"

The constable chuckled, his belly jiggling over his hose. His tunic was stained and dirty, his whiskers unkempt. You would think for the exorbitant fees the man charged he would be better dressed.

"Throw 'em in."

The guards shoved him into the cell, and John looked around his new accommodations.

Anger coursed through him as John realized this had

been planned for a while. For there was already a bed with linens and blankets, table and bench, eating utensils and dishes, and a ewer and basin to wash. They had plenty of time to prepare for his arrival.

The anger dissipated as worry took its place. Had Archie also betrayed the location of their camp? The king's soldiers would kill everyone under his care. It annoyed him to ask this man for anything, but he needs know.

"Will any of my men be joining me?"

The constable turned around, and the grin on his face made John clench his fists.

"Archie was verra talkative. By now the king's men will have destroyed your wicked camp in the wood. Orders were clear. Kill them all."

Eyes blazing, the rage in his belly warming him, John swore viciously. "I will see every one of them dead."

The man sneered at him. "Nay, you'll be dead. Seems you won't be staying with us long. Lord Denby has the ear of the king, and you will die three days from now."

John swore in every language he knew. He cared not for his own life, but with the knowledge he was responsible for so many deaths, he would never forgive himself.

Chapter Five

This morn, like every one since John arrived at the tower, he woke to the sound of metal scraping against metal. The guards banging on the bars with a metal cup as if they were all animals in a cage. At least his gold provided a warm meal. The routine was monotonous, and John took to marking a line on the wall each day. The constable was misinformed. For he did not die in three days. No, he bided his time, waiting for the king's pleasure to give the order. More likely Denby was the cause.

After a se'nnight, John was weary of the dull days. When he heard the keys, he stood waiting, pulling his cloak around him. He would not grant Denby the satisfaction of hearing he had taken ill with fever.

"Rabbie. What are you doing here?"

The boy waited until the guard retreated down the corridor before he spoke. The lad tried to be brave, but his eyes leaked, the anguish on his face warning John of terrible news.

"Gone. They are gone."

Fear dug its claws into his heart. "Who is gone?"

"Soldiers came. So many. They burned our home." He hiccupped. "They killed everyone. Even the babes."

The boy met his gaze, and John had the feeling he was looking into the eyes of an old man.

Rabbie whispered, more to himself than to John, "They killed Magda. She was tending the sick. Soldiers chained the door and fired the hut." He dried his face on a dirty, torn sleeve.

"I've never heard such screams. 'Twas awful."

A blade sliced through John's battered heart. Magda had been with him from the beginning. 'Twas she who found him wandering in the wood, half-dead after being attacked by a group of bandits. He could no more imagine a world in which she did not take breath as he could believe the sky green and the grass blue. Silently, John vowed he would avenge her. In this life or the next. He handed the boy a cup of ale.

"They will be missed. Tell me how you escaped?"

Rabbie sniffled. "I'd gone fishing for supper. I heard the screams and smelled the fire. I hid like you taught us."

John thought the wretched look on the boy's face

must look like his own. He laid a hand on the boy's shoulder.

"'Twas the right course. The soldiers would have cut you down. Know I will avenge our people."

Rabbie looked at him with hope in his eyes. "Do ye have a plan to escape? I can help."

The boy looked around to make sure they were unobserved. Then he reached behind him down the back of his breeches. He grunted and pulled out a cloth-covered bundle. When he opened it, John saw the pouch within. He stifled a chuckle.

"Nasty guards searched me but didn't find it."

John opened the bag, the gold gleaming in the candlelight.

"You did well." John placed the bundle within his cloak. He could use it to bribe one of the guards. At eight years old, the boy had seen a lifetime of tragedy, and yet he was as brave as a warrior.

"I would have died if you hadn't saved me when I was a babe. There must be a way to rescue you from the tower. To repay you for all you have done."

"No. You cannot. You will leave and you will live. That will be repayment."

The small boy had shown such courage that John had to do something for him. What he was about to say might set into motion events he wasn't ready to face. But John would do what needs be done.

"What I am about to tell you, you must swear not to

tell another soul."

The boy's eyes were huge as he nodded.

"I have a brother. His name is Robert Thornton. Lord Highworth. Highworth Castle is near Sutton on the Celtic Sea." John thought for a moment. "You will be safe there from the fighting. Robert will take you in. You can work in the stables. You are good with the horses."

The boy hopped back and forth from one foot to the other.

"You are a Thornton? Your brothers are very powerful. They will come for you. I will take a message to Lord Highworth."

"No." The reply came out sharper than he intended. John took a deep breath and tried again. "Nay, Rabbie. My brothers will lose all if they aid me. You gave your word. Swear you will not speak a word of this to anyone. You will live with Robert and be safe. You will forget me."

Tears ran down Rabbie's face, making tracks in the dirt staining his cheeks. His shoulders slumped. Yet he raised his head and looked John in the eye.

"As you wish, my lord. I will not utter a word to anyone. I swear I will carry your secret to my grave."

"There's no need to call me *my lord*," John said gently. "My title was stripped from me long ago, lad."

John roughly pulled the boy to him, ruffling his hair.

"Live, Rabbie. Make the most of life. You deserve better than the life of a bandit."

The boy clung to him, his tears wetting John's tunic.

"I will never forget you. Never forget all you have done for me." He wiped his nose on his sleeve. "And I will light a candle for those we have lost."

John banged on the bars and listened to footsteps approach. The guard opened the door and Rabbie walked through it. He turned to look at John, nodded once, and disappeared down the corridor. The key turning in the lock sounded final.

If only he could have moved his people sooner. Saved them. Drowning in a sea of grief, John hung his head, the tears silently hitting the stone floor.

Anna didn't know how much time had passed when she opened her eyes. But at least the storm had finally passed. How she could fall asleep when she was scared was beyond her, but she was thankful she didn't have to hear the storm. It was difficult to see in the gloom. Were those people moving around? Was it morning and she was actually in a part of the tower that allowed visitors?

Odd. She didn't remember lights that looked like torches on the walls.

"No way those were there before."

The sound of a throat clearing made her jump.

"Who's there?"

A moan to her right sounded so real it had to be fake.

"Very funny. Ha ha. Good sound effects."

Anna peered into the darkness. "I know we're going to be in trouble for being here after hours."

"Are you lost, demoiselle?"

Chapter Six

Anna stepped back from the cell. "Before the storm I was standing in that very room and it was empty."

Was she having some kind of an out-of-body experience? It was damp here, so there must be mold and the spores were causing her to hallucinate. Inside the formerly empty room was a man. Dressed in period clothing, he was seated at a table with what looked like bread and a goblet. There was a bed in the room, and as she stood there with her mouth open, other sounds reached her ears.

The sounds of voices. Yet none of them sounded happy. These were the sounds of broken men.

"Are you part of the tour? Do people pay extra for this experience?" She tried to see out the small window in the cell. It was dark. "You're way past schedule. This place has been closed for hours."

No. There was nothing in the brochures, and the way she'd found this place...no way they'd let tourists move through secret passages. So what was his deal?

"How did you get in there?"

The man chuckled. "The king's men provided my accommodations. All of us are awaiting our deaths." He stalked over to stand in front of her.

Was the door locked? He might be some kind of psycho.

"The guards are occupied playing cards and will soon be in their cups. They did not bring you in to please them. I ask you again, lady. How did you come to be here?"

Anna swallowed and took a step back. The tone of his voice made her look around for help. He might be locked up, but she was feeling like the one in a cage.

Her teeth started to chatter. "I got lost and somehow came through the passageway that brought me here. But there was no one here before the storm."

"I can assure you, lady, I have been here a fortnight and this is the first time I have seen one such as you. For I would remember your face."

She slowly turned in a circle, peering into the other cells. Each one contained a man. Some looked worse off than others. They looked and smelled very authentic. What was happening? Something was very, very wrong.

"I'm not sure what you're doing here, but I have to

go."

The man peered at her through the close-set bars. He had long blonde hair down to his shoulders and kind brown eyes. Anna sucked in a breath as she got a good look at his face. The guy could rival any movie star in the looks department. Her breath whooshed out and relief flooded through her veins.

"I must have fallen asleep. You're filming a movie, aren't you?" Now it made sense why there would be people here after hours. A rational explanation always made her feel better. She looked around but didn't see any cameras or any movie-looking people. Had she ruined their shot? Maybe they were on a break.

The man took a step back. "Are you unwell? I have heard tales of prisoners here who have lost their wits. Perchance you are lost and should go back to your cell, lady."

Replaying the words over, making sense of what he said, Anna scowled.

"I'm not crazy. And I'm certainly not wasting another moment talking to you." She spun on her heel then faltered. How did she get out? There wasn't a lighted exit sign anywhere.

The chuckle she heard infuriated her. Anna rarely lost her temper. She couldn't remember the last time she was really angry. But something about this man made her furious. She knew she wasn't much to look at, but did he have to be such a jerk? Making fun of her looks and saying he'd remember her face. And what was up with the "wits" remark? Just because you got lost didn't mean you were crazy.

It seemed to be getting warmer. Anna stomped back over and pointed at him through the bars.

"You listen here: just because I ruined your scene doesn't mean you have to be such a jerk. It isn't nice to call someone crazy. I'm having a really bad day."

Instead of throwing something, she took a couple of deep breaths and looked to the end of the corridor. There were torches burning on the walls, and as the light flickered she made out another door. It was open.

At this point she didn't care if they arrested her for staying in the tower after hours. Or for ruining whatever movie they were shooting down here. Movie stars. Arrogant, good-looking jerks.

"My apologies, lady," came the soft voice.

Why did his voice have to sound so sincere? She stopped.

He spoke again. "The ring of keys hanging on the wall. Take them and set me free. I will help you find your way back to wherever you need to go. You have my word."

The keys hung on an old black iron ring. They looked old, and she had to give the movie people credit. Everything looked authentic. She loved going to the movies. But Anna always refused to watch the behind-the-scenes specials. No sense in ruining the magic.

Instead, she liked to believe everything just happened. There was something about knowing how it was done that took all the fun out of it. Made it harder to suspend belief.

This man sounded like he could help, and given her bad luck so far in trying to find the exit, she could use some help. He might be a spoiled movie star, but she was willing to accept his offer if it got her out and on the way back to her hotel. All she wanted was a bubble bath, a pizza, and a gallon of root beer.

The keys were heavier than they looked.

"Wow, I would've thought they'd been made of plastic."

"Plastic? Lady, you speak strangely."

"Whatever." Anna stuck her tongue out at him. "Keep making fun of me and I'll leave you here."

He hadn't made a move to open the door. Would the movie people really lock the actors in the cells in between scenes? Maybe it helped them stay in character. Who knew? She didn't have a clue what went on during the shooting of a flick. Though didn't the guy in those *Lord of the Rings* movies sleep with his sword outside during filming? From what she'd read, actors were an odd bunch.

The first key didn't fit the lock, so she tried the second and third. The fourth one clicked and turned easily.

"I didn't think I'd ever find the right key. You would

think they'd all be the same."

The door swung open and he put a finger to his lips. "Quiet. We must leave without being heard."

Okay, she'd play along. Anna pursed her lips and stood back to let him out. He was really tall. She only came up midway to his chest. Typical movie star—he had the most perfect physique. Muscles in all the right places, and that gorgeous, to-die-for face. And the voice. His voice rasped over her and made her feel all warm and comfy inside. He must be six foot or six foot two. And, of course, he was the total stereotypical blonde god. The kind of man who would never look twice at someone like her.

A perplexed look on his face, he pointed to the door. "Shall we go, mistress?"

"Yes, let's." She made a face at his back and followed him through the doorway into the gloom.

Chapter Seven

Mr. Hollywood led her down the corridor. The man didn't make a sound. Anna had to give him credit for staying in character. Of course, he was so quiet she almost ran into him when he abruptly stopped. The sound of her breathing seemed loud in the dim corridor. Satisfied with whatever he did or didn't hear, he reached back and took hold of her hand. His hand was large, the calluses rough against her skin. The heat from his touch traveled up her arm and seemed to warm her from the inside out. It was a surprise to feel the roughness of his palm. Anna hated to stereotype, and here she was assuming he would be getting manicures every week, not doing the kind of labor that gave you permanent calluses. Point to Mr. Hollywood.

As they moved through the passageways, she

occasionally heard the sound of voices and, even more disturbing, plenty of moans and screams. The guy was definitely going out of his way to avoid anyone. Was he really trying to stay in character, or was he some kind of movie set crasher? Rolling her eyes, Anna knew her imagination was getting away with her. Likely the crew was filming in another part of the tower and he didn't want to ruin the shots. How much did it cost to make a movie here after hours? The insurance costs alone must be astronomical.

As he led her through an archway, the light glinted on his hair and she clapped a hand over her mouth to keep from asking where he got his hair done. Talk about highlights women would fight over. Bet his hairdresser made a fortune.

Hopelessly lost, Anna followed Mr. Hollywood. At the next door, he put his ear against the scarred wood, listening. Seemingly satisfied, he pushed the door open. The smell of water and something rotten filled her nose. They stood at the top of a set of stone stairs leading down to the water.

"I know where we are. We're beneath St. Thomas's Tower. This is the Traitor's Gate. You probably studied up on the tower for your role, but did you know this is where they used to bring the prisoners before imprisoning them in the tower? It's one of the most famous sights here. Can you imagine the feeling of sitting in the boat knowing you were going to be locked up here?"

Mr. Hollywood looked over his shoulder at her as if she were a silly child.

"Aye. I know what it is to be locked in the tower. To pay for the privilege. Charged outrageous fees for food and lodging. All while waiting for your head to leave your shoulders. Or mayhap hanged, then drawn and quartered. I have had much time to consider. I would prefer to escape and avoid either choice."

"Geez, touchy, aren't we? Somebody didn't get a heart drawn on their coffee today."

The man ignored her and let out a soft whistle. She heard the sound of oars slapping water as a man in a boat appeared. Mr. Hollywood had a conversation with the man, something about taking him down the Thames. The sound of the gate opening was her cue to go. Guess he was staying in character. Anna turned to make her way out of the tower. It was dark. How long had she been inside?

"Thank you for showing me the way out. I have to get back to my hotel, not to mention I'm starving."

His response was lost in the noise. She heard the sound of footsteps and what sounded like metal scraping against metal. When she turned around to look, Anna's mouth dropped open. There was a group of five or six men, brandishing swords and running straight for them. They didn't look plastic.

Rooted to the spot, she watched as they came closer

and closer. The next thing she knew, Anna was no longer touching the ground. Mr. Hollywood swept her up in his arms, climbed in the boat, and they were off down the river. If she were directing, this was where she'd have the hero give the heroine a big smooch. Too bad real life wasn't like the movies.

"Wow, that was exciting. But you can stop acting now."

The wind blew the right side of her hair up. There was a pinch on the back of her hand. Anna jerked her hand off the side of the boat to see she was bleeding. There was an arrow embedded in the side of boat.

She wiped the blood on her jeans. At least it was just a scratch. Who used real arrows in a movie? Idiots. "That's taking things a bit far, don't you think?"

Nothing made sense. The feeling that something was horribly wrong came back stronger than ever. As the boat silently slipped through the water, she looked around. Where were the lights? The cars? London looked the same, yet different.

"You are injured." A ripping noise shattered the quiet. He'd torn a piece of his shirt and wrapped her hand. "You aided me. You have my thanks, lady. Once we are away, I will take you wherever you needs go. I keep my word."

The words were coming out of his mouth, but she was having a hard time processing what he was saying. The voice in her head kept screaming she was no longer in present-day London, but she couldn't believe it. Breathing in shallow gasps, she went over every second. Starting from the moment she found herself locked in the tower.

The locket. Where was it? Anna checked all her pockets and came up empty. Had she dropped it? She couldn't have imagined it, could she? When she opened her hand, the scratches on her palm and wrist were still there. She let loose a sigh of relief.

As much as she wanted to believe the man sitting next to her was an actor, a terrible feeling swept through her. Every explanation she could come up with didn't ring true. And she realized it was because of the lack of modern-day sights. Streetlights, vehicles, people milling about. Electric light. All missing. Everywhere she looked, the city was basically dark. And what light she could see seemed to come from torches or candles. Not a single rumble of a truck or horn of a car.

When all else failed, one must believe the most rational explanation. Somehow she had traveled through time.

Anna didn't know how long they were in the boat.

Her phone was also missing, not that it would have done her any good. It was weird not knowing what time it was. The boatman let them off, and she took Hollywood's hand and blindly followed him down the dark street.

The smells reinforced the fact she was no longer in the twenty-first century. She seemed to be watching a movie in which she was one of the characters. Maybe she was in shock or her mind had simply decided to shut down, unable to deal with what was happening. As Anna stepped in a big pile of poop, she smelled horses. The guy led her to some kind of rickety-looking stable. Coins clinked together, a man with no teeth grinned at her, and her feet left the ground again as he lifted her up on a horse. He settled in behind her and they rode off into the night.

After what seemed like hours, the fog in her brain started to clear.

"Why were you...in the tower?"

He started as if he'd forgotten she was sitting right in front of him. The warmth of his body against her back made her drowsy. Anna had the sensation of no longer being rooted to the earth. That any moment the fragile string would snap and she would float off into the clouds.

"I stand accused of treason. Of speaking against my king."

Anna rolled her eyes. "Where I come from, half the

country would be imprisoned."

He chuckled then exhaled sharply. His thighs clenched as he shifted positions.

"Are you hurt?"

"Broken rib, courtesy of the king's soldiers. Never fear, lass. I'm on the mend."

The ease with which he rode, the inflection of his words, the accent, and what sounded like some kind of French before he realized she didn't speak French and switched to English. Not to mention his clothing...all those things added up and reinforced the fact she had somehow traveled back in time.

The only question was *when*. He already thought she was some kind of escaped lunatic. She had to tread carefully. This man was her only connection to this world. And Anna needed him. There was no way she could stay in the past. She had serious obligations waiting for her. The well-being of her dad was at stake.

While she was on vacation her friends were checking in on her dad. Her first vacation in five years. Why had she let Hattie talk her into going? She should've stayed put. Her dad needed her. She quickly calculated in her head. The fees at the memory care facility were paid through the next month. But after that... If she wasn't back by then, her dad's fees would be due, and without her there to cover them, he wouldn't be able to stay at the facility. No matter what, she had to get back. Panic welled up inside her. The man's hand touched her shoulder.

"Do not fear me." He patted her hard enough on the back to make her almost fall off the horse.

"How about not letting me fall?"

"I gave my word to keep you safe and to aid you."

"You can't help me. No one can."

Chapter Eight

Henry Thornton, Lord Ravenskirk, stomped up the steps and into his hall. He'd run through every knight and able-bodied man in the castle and still his anger burned bright.

"Whilst ofttimes pacing, stomping about, and throwing things is helpful, in this situation I don't think it's doing any good. I know I don't feel better."

"Are you trying to sound like me? Did you not tell me it isn't very nice to mock?" He scowled at his wife. Why did Charlotte have to point out what he already knew?

"My accent is getting better, don't you think? I'm still working on the fearsome scowl." She finished arranging the new chairs in his solar.

He rolled his eyes as he'd learned from his wife. Whilst Henry found it annoying when Charlotte did it, he couldn't wait to use the look on his brothers, especially proper Edward.

"The king refused Edward an audience. Lord Denby has his ear and is set to make trouble for all the Thorntons. I still cannot believe James kept the knowledge from me." Henry snorted. "Robert is the only one who does not yet know John is alive. He is recently returned from his traveling about, and we did not dare trust the news to a message. They are too frequently intercepted. Christian will make the journey to inform him in person. I wish I could be there to see his face. He will likely drink for the next fortnight."

Charlotte took his hand, pulling him out of doors, into the sunshine. She didn't stop until they reached her favorite spot in the gardens. When she pulled him down on the bench, she turned to face him with her serious look.

"You know why James did not tell you about John. He gave his word." She sighed. "I wish Robert would find a wife to settle him down. He seems perfectly content to drink and wench for the rest of his life." She leaned back, tilting her face up to the sunshine.

Henry was struck again by how lucky he was to have found her. He would never admit it, but he believed the fates had sent her from the future just for him. And every day he gave thanks she was by his side.

"Robert will one day find his match. Too bad there aren't any more of you. I think a future girl would be the one to make him change his idle ways."

She laughed. "I'd like to see the look on his face when he meets a girl that doesn't swoon over the infamous Thornton looks and charm."

"But I am the handsomest of them all."

"Of course you are, husband." Her look turned grave. "You would have made the same choice as John. I'm sure he believed it was the best way to keep all of you safe. From what you told me, all that your family lost... can you not understand why he would make the choice he did?"

He made a noncommittal noise in the back of his throat. "Aye. But I have missed him. I would have done all in my power to procure his pardon."

She kissed him on the cheek. "I'm sure he knew. It was probably part of the reason he chose to live the life he has. Think how much he missed all of you. Knowing all of you were alive and well and he couldn't see you. When you see him, you can ask him why yourself."

To see his brother John after so long...the thought made Henry weak in the knees. The old king was dead. It was past time for John to come home. Rejoin the world of the living. Charlotte's sisters, Lucy and Melinda, were married to two of the most powerful men in England. Well, beside the Thorntons. Between the six of them, surely they could come up with a way to aid John?

They had to. For if they did not, his brother would

die a traitor's death.

For the first time in his score and eight years, Henry was grateful for the war with Scotland. For war meant the king would be in need of men and gold, both of which the Thorntons had plenty to spare.

"If the king refuses to pardon John, I will ally with Scotland."

Charlotte turned him in surprise. "Would you truly?"

He shook his head. "Nay. But it does make me feel better to say so."

She held him tight. "I have never seen such devious minds as you and your brothers and my sister's husbands. Not to mention my sisters and I. Between all of us, we will come up with a plan to save John."

Henry hoped so. For he could not bear to lose his brother again. Not after finding out he was alive. A smile spread across his face.

"I cannot believe John is the infamous bandit of the wood. The tale of him stretches from one end of England to the other."

"I'm sure he will have many stories to tell." She started to laugh. "The story Melinda told us, about carrying James out of the wood." She was laughing so hard her eyes leaked. "I would've loved to see the look on James' face when Melinda picked him up."

And with the image in his head, Henry's foul mood blew away on the wind. Charlotte always knew how to make him laugh.

The betrayal from Lord Denby would be paid in full. Letitia had caused enough problems when she was alive, and now it seemed she was still causing problems through her husband from the grave. It was time to put an end to the swine.

Chapter Nine

The smell of woodbine drifted back to John. The strange woman in front of him had been silent since their escape. He could almost hear her thinking. He held in a chuckle as he remembered how angry she was when he called her daft.

Why did she help him?

He meant what he'd said. He might have been stripped of his title and his lands, but he still took his knightly vows to heart. This time a snort escaped. Mayhap not all of them.

"Something funny?"

"Nay, lass. Now that we are away, care to tell me who you are?"

"My name's Anna. Anna Waters."

"John Thornton. At your service, lady."

"You don't have to call me lady. It's just Anna. You said you were locked in the tower for treason." Her voice trailed off. She was such a tiny girl that for an instant he wondered if she was a fairy who'd appeared in the dark tower to save him.

Her slim, delicate hands trembled as she stroked the horse, giving away her mood.

"So I was wondering, what year is it?"

He was glad she could not see the surprise on his face. Mayhap she had escaped from her cell and was addled in the head. Though she didn't seem to be witless.

"'Tis the Year of Our Lord 1331."

He felt her flinch. Her fetching backside nestled in between his thighs made him think of home. A wife and babes. Things he thought he would never have. And no longer deserved.

"You know not what year it is?"

She was silent for so long that John opened his mouth to repeat the question, but she finally spoke. He had to lean forward, straining to hear her. Her voice came out as a whisper on the wind.

"I guess I forgot. I fell and hit my head earlier. Maybe that's why I couldn't remember."

He heard the lie on her lips. John knew when people were telling the truth or not; the skill was useful in dealing with pirates and thieves. She was lying, but to what end? For now he would let her keep her lies until he learned her intentions.

"Where are you from, Mistress Waters?"

She waved a hand about, almost hitting him in the nose. "It's a long way from here. I'm visiting London on holiday."

"Alone? Where is your guard or chaperone? 'Tis not safe for a lady to travel unescorted. There are ruffians about." As he would know, for he was the worst of them all.

Her hesitation told him she was about to spew forth another untruth.

"I'm a grown woman. I can take care of myself. Where I come from, it is not unusual for women to travel alone."

This time she definitely managed to surprise him. "I would like to see such a place. Where women think themselves equal to men."

John grinned, knowing she could not see his face. He could feel anger radiating through her as she twisted in the saddle to look up at him, her cheeks pink and her eyes the color of the woods, sparking with fury.

"I'll have you know, where I come from women are equal to men... Well, we're not paid the same, but we can have our own property, vote, and live as we choose. You'll see, the same will happen here in England."

As the darkness gave way to dawn, he stared at her hair. The first time he'd looked it appeared to be a plain brown, rather like mud, but when the sun lit her hair,

John could see the colors of the forest, the moors, and the gold of the sun all woven throughout the long strands. She wasn't beautiful, but the longer he looked at her the more attractive he thought her to be. There was something within, a light spilling out that changed her plain features, making her beautiful.

"I doubt what you say. Women are weak and needs be protected. They cannot wield swords."

"They may be weaker in some aspects, but in many others they are equal, if not stronger."

He gave thanks she had found him and not another. He had come to have rather odd ideas about the sexes. Views none of his peers would share. Anna Waters intrigued him. He looked forward to learning all her secrets.

"We will agree to disagree, mistress."

"You can call me Anna. I guess since you think men are better than women, I should call you *the great one* or *he who is all knowing*?"

This time he threw back his head and let the laughter escape.

"Either of those would do, but John will be fine."

"Whatever."

He heard her huff, and winced as she slammed the back of her head into his chest. He didn't know what *whatever* meant, but by the way she said it, he knew it was meant to provoke. For the first time in a long time, John found himself interested in a woman. There hadn't been anyone...not since Letitia.

"Are you going to tell me where were going? I don't have time for gallivanting around the countryside. I really need to get back to the tower."

He was incredulous. "You would willingly go back? They would kill you for helping me escape."

"I thought I would sneak in when everyone was asleep. I think I left something behind."

He heard the lie again. What wasn't she telling him? Did she have a lover in the tower? The thought made him jealous of the unknown man.

"Nay. We cannot. The king's men are after us. We are traveling to the one place they would never think to look. Once we are safe then I will see you to wherever you needs go. But not back to the tower. Go back to the tower and you *will* die."

By the stiffness of her body he knew she was displeased. But he would not risk going back. It would take them a fortnight to travel to Blackmoor Castle. Ample time to find out what she was hiding.

Chapter Ten

Anna yawned, not bothering to cover her mouth. She was much too busy trying to find a comfortable spot on the horse. Talk about an aching backside. A spin class had nothing on riding for hours on end.

"Is it safe to stop? Won't these people turn you in?"

"You haven't eaten and we must change horses." He tied a mask over his face, making her blink.

"Is this a robbery?"

"Nay, lady. I am known." He bowed. "The bandit of the wood, at your service."

Skeptical, she bit her lip. "If you say so."

And he was right. One of the women blushed and welcomed him to their home. John purchased bread and ale. The bread had little pebbles in it, and she couldn't stand the taste of beer, but at least the cherries were delicious. Not her normal breakfast of cereal, but it would do. The lack of sleep was a bigger issue. Anna was an eight-hour girl, and only sleeping for three hours wasn't working. At least riding with him, if she fell asleep he wouldn't let her fall off.

The morning eased into afternoon before they stopped by a rushing brook.

"Easy. I've got you. You are unused to riding?"

She would have fallen off the horse if he hadn't helped her dismount. They were so close, his hair brushed her face.

Stretching, she said, "No one rides where I come from. Except for pleasure or sport. It's expensive to keep a horse."

He blinked at her, a speculative look on his face. "Truly? 'Tis a curious place, your home."

Fudge. Oh well, it wasn't like she could take it back. Her ideas and words had to sound strange to him. She needed to blend in. And for the hundredth time Anna wished she'd paid more attention during history class instead of drooling over Reed Worth. History was boring and Reed was a blonde, tanned surfer. He never noticed she existed, but she spent hours doodling their names in her notebook.

Why had she landed in 1331? Why not the 1700s or some other time period? All she could remember about this time was from movies. Fat lot of good that would do. All she remembered was William Wallace had been executed at the beginning of the 1300s, and the big, nasty plague was coming in the next fifteen years or so. She had no clue what was happening now.

That was the thing about living in America. Most of her friends didn't pay much attention to what was happening on the world stage. They were all too busy scrabbling to make ends meet. And given the size of America, most people only spoke English. Whereas in many European countries, given their proximity to other countries, people spoke multiple languages. She never thought about being born and raised in Florida. Spending her whole life in one place. But now? Given the circumstances, Anna wished she could have traveled more. Seen the world. And paid attention in history class. Mr. Adams would be laughing his head off if he could see her now.

This was the first time she'd ever seen a horse up close and personal. The animal finished drinking, and she handed him a carrot they'd purchased from the village.

"I like carrots too. If we keep having to eat bread with rocks in it, you and I will be fighting over them."

The horse twitched an ear, ignoring her while he contentedly chewed his veggies.

"Where you come from there are no horses? How do you travel about the countryside?"

Why did he have to be Mr. McNosy? "We have... carriages."

"Are they not drawn by horses?"

When would she learn to keep her mouth shut? Usually she was as silent as a whore in church, but with him…he made her more talkative than LouAnne Hedgepath. They worked together at the diner, and that girl could talk until your ears bled.

"No."

He was stuck with her. And he'd already called her crazy, so what did she have to lose? It wasn't like he could take her to the local police and have her arrested for witchcraft, given the fact he was an escaped convict.

"No? How do these carriages move?"

She put her hands on her hips. "Look, Mr. McNosy. I didn't get enough sleep and I'm cranky. So back off and let me get a drink." Anna surprised herself. What was it about him? He brought out the worst in her. And yet…it felt good to be bossy. She knelt down and scooped up the water with her hands. It was cold and clear and tasted delicious.

John was watching her with a half-smile on his face. He held out a ceramic bottle and she wrinkled her nose.

"No offense, but I hate ale."

Without a word, he rummaged in the knapsack and held out another of the ceramic bottles to her.

"You can fill this one with water. Though you must take care not to drink water in the villages unless you know 'tis not tainted."

"I'll remember, thanks."

She filled the bottle and drained it. Much easier than trying to cup the water in her palm. The cool water cleared the dust from her throat. It was warm out, and she wished she had a pair of shorts. When she started to stand, he reached out and helped her up. It was a strange sensation having a man so close. At the diner she was invisible. Nothing more than a way for people to get food and drink. They didn't actually see her as a person. Treated her as if she had no feelings. Almost as if she were a robot. To feel the weight of his gaze on her, looking into the heart of her, made Anna uncomfortable. She'd grown used to being invisible.

Chapter Eleven

"We should be going." John patted the horse's neck.

"Could we walk for a few minutes? I'm not used to riding, and I don't know if I'll ever sit without pain again."

The sun shone down on him, turning his hair to shades of gold. It was a beautiful, clear day. Even the air smelled different. Fresh and clean.

He squinted up at the sun. "A few moments. The king's men will be riding hard to catch us."

There was no one in the area. They hadn't passed a soul in the past hour. He saw her looking around.

"We must take care."

"It feels good to stretch."

They walked along the water. John was silent. Content with the quiet. She was tired of watching every little thing she said. Lying was hard. It had never come easy to her. Hattie, her only real friend, was so good at lying that Anna sometimes imagined her friend was really a spy instead of a librarian.

It was exhausting trying to make sure she didn't say the wrong thing. What did she have to lose by telling John the truth? Who cared if he didn't believe her? She wasn't staying in this time. To him she was someone who helped him escape and he owed her a favor in return. The part of her who used to read dreamy romances wished he'd look at her like she'd seen couples in the diner look at each other. They were oblivious to the world, so tuned in to each other that nothing else existed. If he ever looked at her like that, it would be enough to satisfy her and she could go back to her busy life without regret. Maybe.

"You asked why I've never ridden a horse." She paused, not sure how to tell him, and afraid if she didn't tell him she would never gather up the courage to try again.

"I live in America. It's a country. The state I live in is called Florida. It's warm there most of the year, and while I've never seen a horse up close, I've seen plenty of alligators—"

"I have never heard of America. Or Florida."

"It's very far away."

"I've heard tell of alligators. One of my brothers wanted to put them in his moat. But 'twas too cold for the creatures. Are they as fearsome as the stories say?"

"They can be. Where I live, there's a waterway behind the building. A fat old gator calls it home. He's almost fourteen feet long. Animal control has relocated him twice, but he always comes back."

She leaned closer to him. "I think he comes back because I feed him marshmallows and I sing to him."

Before she could tell him her big secret, he roughly grabbed her, throwing her to the ground. "Hey. What's wrong with you?"

"Quiet. We are no longer alone."

He pulled a blade from his waist. The man had plenty of gold to pay for everything they needed. Where had he hidden the gold while he was imprisoned? Did the guards let him keep it? She couldn't imagine they would. Anna opened her mouth to ask, and then shut it as the sound of voices reached her.

"Hand over your gold and jewels and we will let you live. Or die by the order of the bandit of the wood."

Anna peeked through her fingers to see a short, squat man missing several teeth and brandishing a blade in each hand. Instead of fearing for her own life, she worried about her teeth. Would she end up like him? What on earth was she going to do for a toothbrush?

Seriously, you're worrying about your teeth? You should be worried about losing all the blood in your body. Get out of there.

"The bandit, you say?"

John looked annoyed instead of worried, which was crazy, since there were three armed men in front of them. The other two looked even worse than the ringleader.

She'd only been in the past a couple of days and already she looked like she'd rolled in the mud. Was this what she had to look forward to if she was stuck here? How on earth was she going to bathe? The thought of a hot shower almost had her groaning, but the thought quickly left her head as she heard the sound of a fist meeting flesh. When she pulled a double shift, sometimes on weekends after three in the morning, there would be a brawl in the parking lot. By now, Anna had seen enough fights to know the three men against John would be an even match. They looked chunky and unaware of their surroundings, whereas he was like a super spy in a movie.

It was over so fast that Anna had the hysterical thought she was actually in a hospital in a coma and this was all a dream.

But the ringleader was on his back staring at the clouds, his eyes unblinking. His chest no longer moving. The sounds of a small animal in pain made her look around for the critter. It took a few minutes before she realized the sound was coming from her throat. She crawled to the bushes and retched. Over and over, she heaved, as her body seemed to think it could expel the awful images by getting rid of the contents in her stomach. All three men were dead, and she'd watched John kill them. It was nothing like the movies or TV.

Another round of gagging left her sweaty and worn out. A couple of leaves served as a makeshift napkin. Anna finished wiping off her mouth and sat up. It was quiet.

"I want to go home," she whispered, looking anywhere but at the bodies on the ground.

"John?"

"I am here. Are you unwell?"

Her teeth were chattering and she shivered. "I've never...seen anyone...die before."

He picked up the men's blades, made a face, and threw them aside. Time slowed. When she blinked, she was in his arms. He murmured softly in her ear. Words she didn't understand.

"You're cold. 'Tis the first time you have watched a man die?"

A brief jerk of her head was all she could manage.

"It pains me you were witness to violence. Know this. Those men would have killed me and made you wish they had killed you. Never hesitate when a man means you grievous harm. Strike first."

He carried her to the edge of the water and gently sat her down.

"Drink and wash. You will feel better."

The sound of moving water helped calm her nerves. A rancid smell lingered, and Anna discreetly sniffed her skin. She smelled.

"I thought it was just a saying. Fear does have a smell."

Images flooded her head, making her dig her hands into the mud, willing them away. If she'd still had any doubt she was no longer in 2016, the events of the past hour had utterly convinced her. Medieval England. Not only was she stranded an ocean away from home, but she was marooned on an island of time. The thought made Anna want to cry. No tears came. The last time she cried was when she was eighteen. The day she had to drop out of college. And this wasn't nearly as bad as what had happened then.

By the time she'd washed as best she could and made her way back to John, he'd moved the bodies.

"Where?"

"In the brush."

There were now two horses. Anna dubiously eyed the beast.

"If you think I'm going to ride that, you're out of your mind."

He patted the animal. "Never mind her. When we are safe at Blackmoor, I will teach you to ride." He turned on the Mr. Hollywood smile. "I would not deprive you of my fine self. We will ride together."

John lifted her up on the horse. He was brown with a white spot on his ear, and he was softer than she'd imagined.

"Whatever lets you sleep at night."

"Um?" He scratched his head.

"You have a big opinion of yourself."

"I am known and feared across England."

"And yet you ended up in the Tower of London."

"You have me there, mistress."

The feel of his body cradling hers had become comforting. As they rode she started to relax, the adrenaline rush leaving her tired.

"Anna? Is there no war or killing where you come from in Florida?"

"Yes, but it's different. Normal people don't go around killing other people." How did she explain it to him? There were murders, suicide bombers, and other craziness, but nothing like this.

Anna blurted out, "I'm from the future." She sat there horrified.

Chapter Twelve

"There is a boy in the kitchens. Says he was sent to work in the stables and will not leave without speaking to you, my lord." His steward sniffed. "Shall I have the guards throw him out?"

Robert Thornton, Lord Highworth, was tickled to see his crusty steward in even more of a foul humor than usual. He tried daily to ruffle the man and a mere boy had accomplished what he could not? Most curious. "I will see the boy."

It took a moment for Robert to regain his footing. He'd drunk to excess last night. And the night before and the night before that. He wiped the sweat from his brow. It was good to be back home. The past fortnight he'd agreed to Edward's demands and visited a handful of eligible maidens. Found none to his liking and proceeded to drown out their shrill voices with drink. One was too tall, one too short, and one laughed like a dying pig. He shuddered thinking on hearing such a dreadful sound every day for the rest of his life.

In truth, he had no desire to marry. He planned to spend his days drinking, wenching, and wagering on the most foolish things. With no vexing wife to shriek at him from morn to night.

In the kitchens, he found a boy so dirty it was difficult to determine the color of his hair beneath the grime. Robert detested filth. His brothers teased him for how often he bathed.

"You have a message for me, boy?"

The boy blinked. "You look just like him." Then, realizing he was in the presence of a noble, he pushed back from the table and stood up straight.

"I am good with horses, my lord. I was told I would find a place in your stables."

The boy hungrily eyed a platter of food one of the serving girls carried out to the hall.

"What is your name?"

"Rabbie, my lord."

"We Thorntons care naught for titles. I am Robert. Sit and fill your belly." Robert heaped the plate high with food and slid it across the table. The greedy manner in which the child ate made him wonder when the boy had last tasted a decent meal.

"How long have you been traveling?"

"A month. I had no horse, so I walked all the way from London."

"Who said you would find a place here?"

The boy looked up at him, a fearful look on his face. "I canna remember."

Robert narrowed his eyes and leaned across the table.

"Do not lie to me. Tell me the truth or I will lock you in my dungeon until you are an old man. There are rats down there. They feast on small children."

Rabbie gasped. "Truly?"

Robert's lip twitched. The boy looked more interested than fearful.

"Then I shall feed you to the pigs."

"'Twas a man said you needed someone good with horses."

"I know the secret you carry." Robert leaned against the wall, one booted foot crossed over the other. He looked down, flicking a speck of dirt off his tunic. The boy was watching every movement, so Robert casually rested a hand on his sword.

The rigors of the journey caught up to the boy as his face crumpled. "How could you? I swore," he whispered.

This was much better. What was Edward up to? He was like an obstinate woman. He snorted.

"I swear all the time. This secret came from the man who looks like me but not as handsome."

Eyes huge, Rabbie put his head on the table. "I said I

would not tell. He said it would keep you safe. Why would he tell you?" The boy's eyes leaked, leaving tracks in the dirt on his face and puddling on the clean table.

"Out with the tale."

"You won't truly feed me to the pigs?"

"Nay. Speak, boy. I needs be sure you are truthful before I tell you what I know." And this was why he won more wagers than he lost.

The boy stared at his plate for a long time, sniffling and wiping his eyes. When he regained his composure, he directly met Robert's gaze.

"Your brother sent me. I didn't know he was your brother for all those years until he told me in the tower, where I visited him."

What the bloody hell? "The Tower of London. Where my brother is held. Continue."

He'd heard no news. Surely the boy was mistaken.

"We always called him Robin. It wasn't until I visited him in the tower he told me his real name." The boy took a deep breath.

"He said you believed him dead. But he is not. He is the bandit of the wood. Your brother, John Thornton."

Robert leaned against the wall, unsteady. He poured a cup of wine and drained it.

The boy blubbered. "You tricked me. You did not know." He wept. "I have failed him. I swore I would not tell."

Robert strode to the table and patted the boy on the

back. He went sprawling on the floor. Not very hearty, this lad. He reached out a hand and helped the boy to his feet.

"'Twas wicked of me. John will understand." Robert smiled, not letting Rabbie see how much the news distressed him. "No one can resist the Thornton charm or the threat of my pigs."

The boy slid him a narrow look. "He will die an awful death."

So much made sense. John was alive. Robert and his brothers would remedy whatever had happened. His older brother was the bandit of the wood. He could scarcely believe the boy but for the truth on his face. Robert heard Lord Denby had found favor with the king. His gut told him Denby was responsible for his brother's current accommodations.

"John will not die." Robert paced back and forth across the kitchen, his head aching. "You have a place here in the stables. I must dispatch messengers to my brothers. Go and bathe, then come to my solar and tell me the tale from the beginning, when you first met John."

"You want me to wash? 'Tis bad for the humors of the body."

Robert threw his head back and laughed. "Everyone at Highworth Castle bathes."

The boy wrinkled his nose, seeming to have second thoughts. Robert barely resisted the urge to scare him again.

"Go. When you come back clean, I will see you have something sweet to eat.

"Featherton," he bellowed.

The man looked down his nose. "My lord?"

"Send the wenches back to the village. I must send messages to my brothers."

"Shall I send all three back?"

His steward did not approve of Robert's appetites.

"Yes, all of them. I have much to think on."

"As you wish, my lord." The man turned on his heel and glided out of the kitchen.

Chapter Thirteen

John was so taken aback he pulled her off the horse and stood facing her. To watch her face. Though for the moment he simply blinked at her like a dolt.

"The future?" He choked on a bug, realized his mouth was hanging open, and shut it with a snap. The woman was daft. "Perchance there is someone at the tower who is missing you."

She stuck her tongue out at him. "Hilarious. I'm not crazy."

He looked her over. The clothing she wore was unlike any he had ever seen. Lasses did not wear hose as she did. Hers were a dark blue and molded to her plump backside. Every moment they rode, he was aware of her nestled into his thighs.

"Can you prove this outlandish claim?"

She narrowed her eyes at him. "No. I lost my phone and wallet when I traveled through time."

"How did you travel through time? In one of your horseless carriages?"

Against her will, he saw the smile. She stood with her hands on her hips trying to scowl. "No. But you're doing better with the whole sarcasm thing." The wind caught her hair, blowing it across her face. She spat it out.

"Spinach fudge." Anna held up a hand. "I recognize that look. Fudge is a type of sweet, so no one in his or her right mind would put spinach in it. I don't curse like you. I like to make my own words."

"Ah. Sarcasm?"

"Like mocking. Do you have a ribbon or piece of string?"

He poked through the sack holding their belongings and came up with a dirty piece of string.

"Will this do?"

She snatched it. "Perfect."

'Twas an act he thought should only be performed in front of her husband. He wanted to haul her to him and kiss her senseless as he watched her braid her long hair, the tip of her tongue in the corner of her mouth as she went about her task.

"Much better." She bent down, picking a flower. "I don't know how I fell through time. I was walking through the tower and went into your cell. There was a storm and lightning. When I woke, there you were."

"What year did you come from?"

"Now you will think I'm crazy. It was 2016."

Six hundred and seventy-five years. "Nay. 'Tis not possible."

"And yet here I am."

He had to sit down in the grass before he fell down. John had seen many strange things in his thirty-two years, but none such as the woman in front of him. Though there was something about her...the way she spoke that reminded him of someone.

"Tell me of this future. Who is king?"

"America doesn't have a king. Or a monarchy. We have a president. Here in England, a queen is on the throne but the monarchy no longer has the power it does now."

"A queen on the throne? I should live to see such a sight."

"She's a good ruler. The carriage I told you about? It's called a car. Made of metal and requiring no horses. It moves on its own."

"What do you feed this metal beast?"

"Something called gas or electricity. You can travel hundreds of miles in a single day."

His mouth dropped open again. "Nay." To see such wonders.

"And we can fly."

He looked at her shoulders.

"I don't have wings. We climb aboard a plane, a

metal flying bird, and can travel from England to France in less than an hour."

John felt faint. He could not imagine such doings.

"Men have walked on the moon."

He looked to the heavens. "Anna. You must never tell anyone what you have told me. Many would burn you for a witch or lock you away, sure you are mad."

"Why do you think it's taken me so long to tell you? Do you believe me?"

"I...I want to believe you." The truth was in her eyes. She believed she came from the future. Mayhap she was mad. It would make life simpler if she was mad. The future. The marvels she spoke of, no wonder she wanted to go home.

He stood, swayed, and looked to the sky again. Men flying through the air. "We have tarried overlong."

"Thank you for listening. I know I sound crazy, but I swear on my dad, I'm telling you the truth." She let him lift her onto the horse. "My dad needs me. I have to get home."

He needed time to think. "Is there aught else you would tell me?" Heaven help him if she said yes.

"No. Isn't that enough?"

"Saints be, 'tis more than enough."

It would be dark in a few hours. As they rode, he thought what it would be like if she were his. If she was mad? No matter, he still wanted her.

Chapter Fourteen

Each day they rode, Anna admired the scenery and hoped they would find someone to purchase a hot meal from. In her own time, she was inside a lot. Working three jobs did that, so at first all the time outdoors was fun. After several days it became monotonous and she dreamed of cars and trains. Being on a horse all day was very different from being on her feet all day.

At night they slept wrapped up in blankets on the ground after a meager dinner. The night before, when they slept in a barn after a hot meal, it had rivaled staying in her hotel in London. The days passed and the landscape changed. Fog rolled in. Anna kept imagining werewolves running across the creepy moors.

She didn't date much, had never spent so much time alone with a man. No distractions of any kind. There was something to be said for no phones. They had time to really get to know each other. He told her how he became the bandit, and some of his funnier adventures. Like the carriage they held up thinking they would find gold inside. Instead the woman inside had two pigs with her, both wearing jewels and dressed up.

Being an outlaw explained why he knew the men he killed were lying. At least since that terrible experience happened almost two weeks ago, they hadn't run into any other thieves. And still no sign of the men chasing them. She hoped they'd gotten tired of the chase and gone home.

"Won't the king send men to your home? Wouldn't it be the first place they look for us?"

"I lived there a long time ago. The men would not think me so daft as to go home. 'Twill buy us time to find somewhere safe."

What was that smell? It had been with them since yesterday. She sniffed the horse. No, he smelled like a horse. Leaning back, she turned her head and smelled John. Yuck. He was part of the bad smell, but not all of it. No. It couldn't be.

Discreetly, she lifted her arm, playing with her hair. Anna turned her head and sniffed at her armpit.

"This is worse than a pool full of alligators. I stink."

The rumble behind her made Anna flinch.

"I said that out loud, didn't I?"

His chest vibrated against her back, but to his credit

he didn't laugh out loud.

"Aye. You smell fine to me." He purposely sniffed at her. "Forgive me. We are almost to Blackmoor. I will find you something more suitable to wear."

She was prevented from answering as it started to pour just like an afternoon thunderstorm in Florida. The clouds hung low, silver against the gray sky. If she were warm and dry in a train or a car, she would appreciate the storm. The scene was one of rugged beauty. Lonely and windswept. The word *melancholy* came to mind.

Anna laughed hysterically. "All we need now is for Heathcliff to ride across the moors."

His breath was warm against her ear.

"I know no one named Heathcliff. The moors can be dangerous. The ground treacherous, and the bogs deadly. Do not make your way through them alone."

Could the man read minds? She'd been trying to pay attention, mark rocks or other signposts along the way. As good as she was with directions, she had to admit it looked dangerous. The horse shook his head, nervous, but John kept a firm grip on the reins and guided the beast through the storm. How he could see the trail was beyond her. All she could see was mud. And then something loomed in the distance, making her shiver.

"That's a castle." She twisted in the saddle to look at him. "You didn't tell me you lived in a castle."

"Does it make a difference?"

"I guess not. Certainly didn't expect a big, honking

castle." The rain chilled her, or maybe it was the monstrosity in front of her. Talk about the perfect backdrop for a horror movie.

"Blackmoor Castle has been in my family a long time. 'Twas given to me by my father." She heard the laughter in his voice. "'Tis rumored to be haunted. Though I never saw a spirit."

"Oh, great. Like that's supposed to make me feel better."

Some long-forgotten lecture from history class, or maybe from a book she'd read back when she actually had time to read, popped into her head.

"Wait a minute. You said your name is John Thornton. Shouldn't you be Lord Blackmoor or something fancy?"

After spending twenty-four hours a day, every day, for the past two weeks with the man, she heard the sadness in his voice. Given her job, she was good at reading people. Could tell who would tip and who wouldn't. Who would skip out on the check and who would be a total pain in the butt.

"Nay. I haven't been Lord Blackmoor in a long time. When my lands and gold were confiscated, my title was stripped from me. My older brother, Edward, won back the castle. It has been empty ever since."

He shifted in the saddle. She felt the tension radiating off his body. The stiffness of his legs and body against her own.

"Prepare yourself. Blackmoor may be in need of repair."

"It can't be any worse than sleeping outside on the ground. At least we'll have a roof over our heads to shelter us from the rain."

As the looming stone fortress grew larger, a twinge of jealousy burned through her. He was only nine years older than her, yet he owned a freaking castle and had a bag of gold. She worked a full-time job and two part-time jobs, and still Anna could barely make ends meet after paying the memory care facility fees. To have her own place. Know there was enough money to ensure your security. No more worries. Then she felt like a brat. Here she was being a green-eyed monster, and if he was captured, he'd die for committing treason. In her whole life, she'd never even had a parking ticket.

"So where exactly are we? It's not like there any signs."

"We are in the middle of the country. York is to our east." He stopped speaking, his body stiff as they rode across a bridge through a scary-looking archway with a metal gate above their heads. The gate had spikes at the end. In the horror movie, the gate would come down and impale a helpless victim. They rode into a courtyard. It was so quiet Anna looked around, half expecting at any moment to hear rattling chains and the moaning of ghosts.

His voice came out as a croak. "'Tis deserted. I

thought perchance a few of my servants would've stayed on, or Edward would have made sure there was a caretaker."

It looked like the castle was falling down. Like one of the many ruins she had seen in the guidebooks and didn't even get to see, since she'd only been in London two days when she, like Alice, fell down the rabbit hole.

Did time move the same in the past as it did in her own era? She hoped not. If it did, she'd been gone three weeks. Hattie would be frantic. What had she thought when Anna wasn't on the flight home? In this situation, it was a small mercy her poor father no longer knew who she was. He wouldn't miss her. Though he might wonder why the girl who came to read to him twice a week no longer visited.

"Is it safe to stay here? Are you sure the soldiers won't come here looking for us?"

"We will have a se'nnight at most. Enough time to decide where to go."

The door opened. A man peered out through the rain at them.

"Who's there?"

"John Thornton. I've come home."

Chapter Fifteen

The man standing in the doorway was bald and hunched over. He gazed up at John through light blue eyes. There was intelligence in his gaze. The man shuffled back to allow entrance to the hall.

"Come back from the dead, have ye? Best come in afore someone sees ye." Without waiting for an answer, he shuffled into the gloom.

Haunted. Over the years he'd heard the rumors. Blackmoor Castle haunted by demons and ghosts. People traveling went out of their way to avoid the castle, crossing themselves as they moved across his lands. As far as he knew, there'd never been a sighting of a ghost. He'd encouraged the rumors over the years, wanting to keep people away. If he couldn't live at Blackmoor, he didn't want anyone else walking through his hall, sleeping in his bed.

They followed the man to the kitchens. Long-buried feelings of family and home made him want to weep like a babe. The utter disrepair and ruin made him regret the actions of his youth. Something wet landed on his nose. Looking up, he saw a great, gaping hole in the roof.

"Is there no one else here?"

"Some left after you were arrested. Others waited, hoping the lord would return. When your brother sent word you were dead, most of the others fled. Your brothers promised to take care of every man, woman, and child. Many went to their estates. I stayed. You know the tales?" The man looked over his shoulder, a twinkle in his eye. "They say Blackmoor 'tis haunted by the very devil himself."

"Have you seen the devil?"

"Only the one following me." The old man scratched his arse as he muttered. He and Anna sat at a bench, the wood creaking under their weight. John hoped he would not suffer the humiliation of Anna seeing him sprawled on his backside. The man limped over, a platter in one hand, a jug in the other.

"The larder is empty." He patted a ring of keys around his waist. "I kept the wine locked away. Plenty to drink."

As he ambled out of the room, he said, "I'll ready your chamber."

Ten long years had passed since John had been

home. He watched Anna looking around, noticing the dirt and ruin, saw the worry on her face. She seemed to sense him looking at her. Turning green eyes on him, she arched a brow.

"A bit of a fixer-upper, huh?"

He understood the meaning behind the strange words. "Blackmoor has withstood battles. A few holes in the roof won't bring the walls down. Mayhap we will have company in our beds."

"What? Like bedbugs? Rats?" She was as skittish as a filly. "We don't have castles where I come from. There are big houses, but nothing like this."

And something about the way she said it made him pause. He always assumed his home would stand for hundreds of years, long after he'd turned to dust. To think it no longer stood in her time cracked the ice he'd built around his heart so long ago. What had happened to Blackmoor? Did it fall to his enemies?

"There are no more castles?"

Anna touched his arm, the heat of her touch warming him from inside.

"Where I come from there were never castles to begin with. There are many castles in England and other countries. Though I don't know if Blackmoor is still standing. I'd only arrived in London two days before I ended up here. I didn't have time to see the countryside."

She reached up to wipe rain from her face. It was

raining harder outside, thunder in the distance.

Anna knocked the platter onto the floor. "Sorry. There was a terrible storm when...everything happened. I've never liked storms." She nibbled a bit of cheese, her hand trembling.

"I do know the Tower of London stands. As do Buckingham Palace and Westminster Abbey." She wrinkled her nose, thinking. "Forget what I said about Buckingham Palace. It hasn't even been built yet. It was built in the early 1700s, if I remember my history correctly."

He was curious about her time. Wanted to know more. "When did a queen take the throne?"

She bit her lip, which he found rather fetching. "Queen Mary was the first. Sometime in the mid-1500s."

He tried to accept the knowledge a woman held the throne and did not have absolute power. "Why does your country not have a ruler?"

"People from Europe came to America to get away from the monarchy. We have a president and congress. But it's not like anyone can order your head chopped off because you made them mad."

Her eyes turned the color of moss when she laughed.

"Though I think I'd like to be queen. It would be nice to say *off with their heads* and get rid of anyone I didn't like."

"You're rather bloodthirsty for such a small slip of a girl, Anna Waters."

She blushed. He reached out to stroke her cheek then snatched his hand back. He was a wanted man and would likely not live long. He could not afford to open his heart to a woman. Especially one who claimed to be from the future. She would return to her own time, where he had been dead and turned to dust for hundreds of years. Would she marry? The thought of another man touching her made him want to throw something.

The steward returned. "The rats have been at the bedding."

"Wonderful. And I thought cockroaches were bad," Anna muttered as she bit into the bread.

John fought to keep a straight face. "I must confess, I do not remember your name."

The man scratched at his whiskers. "I suspect I had a bit more hair then. My name is Emory. My father and brother served ye as well."

The memory came back. A slight man with hair as black as night. Piercing blue eyes, all of them. John recognized the eyes.

"My apologies. I remember now. You took good care of me and have my gratitude for staying."

"Where would I go? I was born here. Lived here all my life, and I will die at Blackmoor."

He motioned for them to follow. "The chamber is this way."

Emory led them through the hall and up a flight of

stairs. Memories flooded John's thoughts. A small part of him wished circumstances were different. He wished to rebuild his home. See his brothers. And perchance to find a woman to care for him. But that was not to be his life.

They reached the chamber, and Emory opened the door.

"Won't be much for supper tomorrow, but I'll see what I can do." He left them standing in the room.

"Is my room across the hall?" There was a strange look on Anna's face, and it took John a moment to realize why.

"Remain here." He quickly crossed the hall and opened the door to the other chamber. There was a great, gaping hole in the wall and he could see outside to the trees. The other two chambers were in even worse repair. He came back dusting his hands on his hose.

"This is the only chamber. I will sleep on the floor."

She looked horrified. "The stone is cold. You'll get sick." Turning to face the bed, she said quietly, "We slept next to each other while we traveled."

"'Twas different."

"No, it wasn't. You said you were a knight, so I will expect you to behave honorably and we will share the bed."

He reeled back. "Nay, we cannot. You are not wise to trust my intentions. I have been a bandit as long as a knight."

"Whatever. Why can't we share?"

"People will talk. Your reputation is at risk."

"There's no one here but Emory, and I don't think he cares. Anyway, it's not like you're going to ravish me or anything."

The thought had not crossed his mind until she said it. John could well imagine them together. Her long hair spread over the pillow, shimmering in the candlelight. A rosy hue to her skin as he brought her pleasure. He shifted from foot to foot.

"Nay. I would not think to lay a finger upon you."

Was it his imagination or did she look distressed by his words?

"I will sleep in the kitchens. Sleep well, Anna." He left her standing there.

Chapter Sixteen

The next day, they explored John's home. At least she was able to wash her bra and hang it to dry before she went to sleep.

The bed was lumpy, and she dreamt bedbugs crawled over her, but other than that she slept well. When John told her he'd never lay a finger on her, at first she wanted to cry. Then she wanted to smack him, and finally, she accepted he wasn't attracted to her like she was to him.

When she had a few moments alone, she threw her undies in the fire. The elastic was coming apart and there was a hole in the side. For the first time since she'd moved from diapers to underwear, Anna went without. Exhausted, she fell asleep in the afternoon and woke to the sound of a soft knock at the door.

"Supper is ready."

She threw her hair up in a ponytail, tying it with the string she'd used on her braid.

"I'm famished."

"Then we shall make haste." Once they reached the bottom of the stairs, he took her hand and led her to the kitchens. He did what many could not. Confused her.

Anna could have kissed Emory. He served them a delicious hot meal. After he hemmed and hawed for a bit, the man finally agreed to eat with them in the kitchen. With the gaping hole in the roof of the hall it would have been like eating outside in a storm. Not to mention there weren't any furnishings, so they would have been sitting on the cold stone floor. In the kitchen, there was a cozy fire in the hearth, they were inside, and she ate off an actual plate. Life was good.

Emory pushed back from the table. "I'll see to the horses, my lord."

"John. Not *my lord*. Not anymore."

The man frowned, muttering.

"Thank you for supper, Emory. It was delicious."

He beamed at her. Anna thought he was in a hurry to get away from them because he was uncomfortable with how casual John was. The steward had tried to call him *my lord* several times, and each time John corrected him. She could understand Emory. He was raised serving the Thornton family and would always think of John as Lord Blackmoor. John, though...he'd lost everything, and she thought the title reminded him of not only the things he had lost but the loss of his family. And ten whole years.

If she were still in modern-day Florida, there was no way Anna would've freed a man from prison. Let alone traveled with him across a country she was unfamiliar with. Here in medieval England, it seemed a perfectly normal thing to do. Her entire life she had been content to sit on the sidelines. To be invisible. Hiding in the corners.

When driving the speed limit, she was nervous when a cop passed her. Now she was a criminal. By the simple act of turning a key in a lock. Would the soldiers arrest her and throw her in the tower for what she had done? Worse, would she pay with her life for a decision made on impulse? Her incarceration certainly wouldn't be all Martha Stewart, knitting ponchos and gathering salad greens.

Treason was serious stuff even in her time. It had to be worse here. Her stomach did flip-flops from thinking about being locked in one of the cells. During their travels, John explained you had to pay for accommodations. Pay for your food, blankets, basically for everything.

She had no money. Nor any jewels. If they locked her up, she would have nothing to offer. And someone without means would die quickly in the tower or face difficult choices. She heard the awful cries as they'd escaped. Anna swallowed, remembering the man she saw lying dead in his cell, eyes open and unseeing. He was dressed in rags, his leg shaking as vermin moved in the dim light. A shudder went through her.

"You are quiet this eve. It is aught amiss?"

"I'm usually quiet. But there seems to be something about you that makes me talk more." And stand up for herself. Knowing he wasn't interested in her made it easy to banter back and forth. Just once, couldn't the hot guy fall for the mousy girl?

She tore the bread on the plate in front of her into small pieces. In the corner of the kitchen, a mouse sat up, whiskers twitching. Before she considered what she was doing, Anna threw him a tiny piece of bread. He grabbed it and scurried into a hole in the corner. She knew she was asking for trouble. Feeding a mouse. Where there was one there were probably hundreds. But he looked so cute and hungry that she couldn't resist. *Run across me while I sleep, though, and I'll be getting a cat, Mr. Mouse.*

"If this is you talking more, mistress. I would hate to see when you are silent." John smiled. He was utterly charming even while he was obviously distracted. She hadn't been the only one quiet tonight. Coming home must make him feel the full weight of his troubles bearing down on him.

"I'm just tired. It's been a long journey."

"I will send Emory for clothes for you tomorrow, and

a bath. Would that please you?"

What would it be like if he turned the full impact of those kind brown eyes upon her and saw her truly for the first time? Part of her wanted to find out. But the other part...

"Very much. I'm afraid if I go too much longer, flies will start following me around."

He grinned. "I would follow you, stench or not."

If only. A girl could dream.

"I know you need to stay away from the tower. And I certainly understand, given the circumstances. But I must find a way back home. I have to believe since I fell through time in the Tower of London, that is where I must go to make my way home."

"And if you cannot go home? Then..."

He seemed almost ready to tell her something and then changed his mind. She shrugged it off.

"I have to stay positive. There are those who need me at home. Depend upon me for their welfare."

He opened his mouth to ask her a question when they heard a commotion in the hall.

John jumped to his feet, sword and dagger in hand.

"Is that any way to greet your brother?"

Chapter Seventeen

Anna couldn't believe her eyes. She was looking at another Hollywood hunk. He looked younger than John. He didn't have the same worries etched across his face. She would've known them as brothers anywhere.

John sheathed his blades and went to his brother, who promptly punched him in the face. Knowing when to get out of the way, Anna sat on the edge of the table as John and his brother exchanged blows. Soon they were rolling around on the floor, cursing at each other. At least, she assumed they were cursing. The words sounded sort of like French. What was it with men and fighting? Maybe it was like women meeting and sizing up each other's appearances.

John brushed the dust from his tunic, blood running down the side of his face. He held out a hand to his

brother.

The guy slapped the proffered hand away. "I am not an infirm lad."

He straightened his clothing and made her a bow.

"Who is this vision of loveliness? A fairy residing in this ruin? Seeing her in your ruin of a hall, I can almost forgive you for letting me think you dead these past ten years."

Heaven help her. He was just as charming as John, if not more so. Though there was something to be said for a man who took his responsibilities seriously. Not that she was falling for John; it was just an observation. His brother looked like what her favorite Regency romance novels would call a rake.

"I'm Anna. Anna Waters."

"Robert Thornton, at your service, lady."

"I can tell you are brothers."

"Yes. I am the more handsome one, wouldn't you agree?"

"Whatever." She laughed at the fake hurt look on Robert's face. John took another swipe at his brother. Then his face turned serious.

"I am sorry, Rob. I wanted to keep all of you safe."

"We will have time to talk later, brother. I am famished."

"There likely isn't enough for your enormous appetite."

"Dolt."

"Whoreson." John waved a hand around the hall. "As you can see, there's a great deal of work to be done."

"'Tis fortunate I am here. Your lady and I would starve otherwise." Robert winked at her and she grinned. He was trouble. "I have brought provisions." Like a magician conjuring a rabbit out of a hat, Anna watched as people streamed through the doors.

"I have brought servants and food. And furniture." Robert looked at his brother as if waiting for him to notice something.

Anna saw the moment it hit John. "My furnishings."

"I cleared out Blackmoor after..." He tucked a lock of hair behind his ear. "I'm sorry I didn't keep the place up."

John clapped his brother on the back.

"Nay, Robert. I am grateful for all you have done. You should not have brought all this. I will not be here long enough. The king's men will come. They will take me back to the tower. And then where will everyone go?"

"You worry overmuch," Robert said softly to his brother.

Anna wanted to leave the hall, leaving them to have a private conversation. She started to inch away but John turned that all-seeing gaze upon her.

"Anna, stay with us."

Robert placed a hand on his brother's shoulder.

"It will not come to that, John. But if it should,

everyone will come back with me. We have all agreed to keep your servants safe. What is family if not to help when there is need?"

"You were so young when our family lost everything. I will not have such a thing on my conscience again."

"'Tis no longer your choice. We will aid you. The old king is dead. Letitia was a silly girl. Lord Denby is a bastard who will get what he deserves. The Thorntons stand together. Edward is seeking an audience with the king. He will ask him to pardon you."

At this Robert grinned. "After all, he is the best of us all at keeping his temper."

The love John and his brother had for one another... Anna yearned to know the feeling. The knowledge you had another in the world that cared for you. A brother or sister who would help you whenever you needed them.

As an only child, she longed for a big, boisterous family. Her first boyfriend after high school came from a family of six brothers. She stayed with him for too long because she loved his family—as it turned out, much more than she cared for him.

She leaned against the wall, sipping a cup of water, content to listen to them talk. Something Robert said made her pay attention.

"We have sent messengers across the land. They report seeing you in York. Others tell the king's soldiers you were spotted in London, and others swear they spoke with you near the border of Scotland." He grinned. "'Twas James' idea."

"He is aiding us?"

"Aye. As is William Brandon."

John's brother filled the room with his presence. She or John didn't have a prayer of getting a word in. Robert practically hopped around the kitchen with glee. Anna couldn't help smiling at the younger version of John. He must give the women around England fits.

"A small band of soldiers came to Falconburg. The Red Knight told them to do something I rather thought was impossible. He learned the saying from his wife, Melinda."

Robert turned to Anna. "You remind me of her. Something about the way you speak."

Weird. She didn't think much of the comment until she saw the look on John's face. He was as pale as the moon. Who on earth was Melinda? A spark of jealously flared. Anna hoped she wasn't an old girlfriend. She didn't want to interrupt, so as soon as she had John alone, she would ask.

"Do not forget, brother, we're at war. The king is in need of gold and men. The years have been good to the Thorntons and to the bandit, from what I hear. We have plenty of both and would offer it gladly to keep you safe and back among us."

John quickly wiped his sleeve across his eyes. "The servants are stirring up dust. I have a bit in my eye."

Robert snorted. "As you will, brother." He looked

around the hall, hands on his hips. "Tomorrow we will drink and feast."

Chapter Eighteen

A hundred times a day or so, it seemed to Anna, she tried to wish herself home. Morning, night, inside, outside. Different days of the week, storms or sunny days. She tried every combination she could think of and nothing worked. So either being at the tower would take her back to her own time or she was stuck here. In medieval England with a man she was falling in love with and who wasn't attracted to her at all.

Almost a month had passed, and with every day, home seemed more of a distant memory. A place she dreamed of with a father who needed her.

"Mistress?"

She jerked up from the pile of hay she'd been sitting in, talking to Brown Horse and Black Horse. So they were awful names, but she hadn't come up with good ones. If she named them, it felt like she was accepting her life here. One more block cemented to keep her here.

"Sorry, you startled me."

The woman—Sara, maybe?—looked like she was in a hurry.

"Come along. Your bath is ready and then the girls will help you dress in more...er, proper clothing."

The servants Robert had brought stared at her filthy jeans and shirt, but none said anything. After hearing of some of Robert's activities, she thought they were pretty jaded to anything shocking.

"A bath would be heavenly."

She patted the horses as she left the stables. They looked so much better. The men had worked on the stable first, saying there wasn't much damage. Right now, the horses had better sleeping arrangements than she did.

When had Robert grown up to be a man? And one so eager to bathe all the time? John was an idiot, so lost in his own problems he had given little thought to Anna wearing the same clothes for weeks. Not once had she complained. Most ladies he came into contact with would've complained long and loudly until he procured what they desired. She never said a word. Washed as best she could. He chuckled. She had been vexed that he laughed when she said she smelled. Spending so much time on the road, one would have an odor. He thought she smelled nice.

John was bewitched by the hose she called jeans. Women did not wear such garments. Mistress Waters was a fetching sight, and he'd scowled at more than one guard lingering about.

"Thinking of the enchanting lass?" Robert smirked. "She will prefer me to you now that I brought her clothing, food, and a bathing tub. And rose-scented soap."

"Nay. She does not like castles. And yours looks like it is a folly the king requested."

"All women like pretty things. Truly she does not care for castles nor titles?" Robert stroked his chin. "She must be the only woman in all the land. I should take a closer look. A woman such as Anna would make a fine wife."

"Touch her and lose your hand." John stretched out in front of the fire, grateful for the chairs his brother had thought to bring along. "You are much too picky and will never find a wife to suit you. You prefer to wager and drink and hunt."

Robert peered into his cup. "Tell me more about

Anna. There is something about her..."

"First, there is something I should tell you. James Rivers and his wife Melinda knew I was alive." Things he thought strange about Melinda suddenly made sense. Why Anna reminded him of someone. Could it be possible?

"What are you thinking?"

"Nothing."

"If James and Melinda know, then so does William Brandon. William is married to Melinda's sister, Lucy." Robert shut his mouth and stared into the fire.

"Out with it."

"You would not have heard. Henry is married."

"Little Henry?"

"Not so little anymore. He married the third sister, Charlotte."

"Bloody hell. How many sisters are there?"

Robert chuckled. "Only the three."

The more John thought on it, the more he was certain. Anna and Melinda were the same. Melinda spoke with a different accent, but Anna said America was a vast country, and there were many accents. Could all three sisters be from the future? Anna assured him people did not travel through time. How did the Merriweather sisters come to be in the past? Did they know how to get back? Perchance they could aid Anna?

Did he want her to go?

"You are thinking so hard 'tis making my head hurt.

Tell me, John. You know I would do anything within my power to aid you."

"Have you noticed anything odd about Melinda or her sisters?"

Now it was Robert's turn to look as if he had a secret. His brother turned his head toward the stairs as if he could peer through the stone.

"The girl dresses strangely."

"She is not a girl. Mistress Waters is a score and three. Anna is different."

"You have been the bandit of the wood for far too long. I am your brother. You can tell me anything." Robert sat there and stared at him, waiting.

John knew he could trust Robert, and yet...after the betrayal of Archie, he found the words lodged in his throat. 'Twas her secret. Did he have the right to tell?

"You asked how I came to meet Anna. Pour the wine and I'll tell you." John added more wood to the fire—the servants were busy, and they were alone in the hall. He leaned back in the chair, fingers steepled under his chin, and gazed at his brother.

"I was thinking of all of you. The dishonor I brought to the Thornton name. When I looked up, she was outside the cell. As if she'd sprung up from the very stone itself."

He looked into the flames, remembering seeing her for the first time, struck by the innocence on her face.

"The guards had been up late and were still sleeping.

She was dressed as you saw her tonight. I asked for her aid. She took the ring of keys from the wall and released me. 'Twas strange; she did not want to leave the tower."

"Was she imprisoned? How did she escape?" Robert was leaning forward in his chair, one booted foot tapping against the stone floor.

"Nay. She was visiting the tower. In her time the tower is a place people come to gaze upon. 'Tis no longer used as a prison."

He waited, watching the words sink in to his brother's mind.

"What do you mean, *in her time*?" Robert paced back and forth in front of the fire. He whirled around to face John. "She said *whatever*. Just like Melinda and her sisters do. Where is she from?"

"The right question would be *when* is she from."

Robert gaped at him. A thoughtful look crossed his face.

John added, "Anna says she is from the future. The Year of our Lord 2016. Did you know in her time, a queen rules over England?"

In the dim firelight, Robert turned the color of marble. He looked unwell. "So many things make sense. I thought the Merriweather sisters odd. But now..."

He looked at John. "Think you they too are from the future? I would very much like to see what the world becomes. Think one of them can travel back to their own time?"

"Nay." John shook his head. "Anna has been most distressed. She needs go home. She has family dependent on her."

"Is she married?" Robert asked. John scowled. "What? I see the way you look at her. You care for her. Why haven't you wooed her?"

"Aye. I do. But I will not have her in danger. With me, Anna is not safe. She is kind and decent and deserves better."

"I would woo her."

John was about to strike his brother when he saw Robert grinning.

"Do I tell Anna about Melinda and her sisters?"

"Who's Melinda?" Anna said as she stepped into the room.

Chapter Nineteen

The tone of their voices stopped Anna from entering the room. John and Robert were speaking in low voices. Standing still, she closed her eyes and listened. While she knew you shouldn't eavesdrop unless you wanted to hear something you might not like, she couldn't help herself.

After a long, hot bath, she felt human again. Two of the women Robert had brought with him helped her undress, gaping at her bra. Their looks had made her so nervous that when they left the room to let her soak, she tossed it in the fire, happy she was small-chested. At least if she put her old clothes back on, it wouldn't be too obvious she wasn't wearing a bra.

The steam rose up around her, making her drowsy. The women bustled in, soaping and washing her hair.

Bits of leaves, twigs, and straw floated in the tub. It was heavenly to feel and smell clean again. The dress they provided was stunning. A deep brown with embroidery at the bottom and all over the sleeves. She felt like a princess. One of the women dubiously eyed her clothes, saying she'd launder them. Anna wondered if they were headed for the fire.

A younger girl had braided her hair, tying the end with a gold velvet ribbon. Anna felt beautiful for the first time in a long time.

John raised his voice. She caught something about someone named Melinda. Did he have a girlfriend? He hadn't mentioned one so far. Why would someone as good-looking and rich as him want someone as poor and plain as she? He had been nothing but kind to her. Gave her no indication he had deeper feelings. He was a knight before becoming a bandit and was helping her. Even if he was the first man who had ever looked at Anna like he saw her for who she was. A person of value.

Smoothing her hands over the dress, she took a deep breath and stepped into the room. "Who's Melinda?"

They both stared at her, their mouths hanging open. Robert recovered first.

"A vision of loveliness. Methinks you are a fairy princess come to live among the humans." He pretended to swoon.

She laughed, not believing a word he said.

"Sit here by the fire. Away from my dolt of a brother."

John helped her to the chair. They sat after she did.

"You are the most beautiful woman in the realm, mistress."

Robert was a total playboy. "Please, call me Anna."

"Then you must call me Robert."

He slid John a look. One Anna had seen between the brothers of her ex-boyfriend. It always meant one of them was about to tease the other one. And they would usually end up rolling around on the floor punching each other.

"Are you married?"

"No. Why do you ask?"

"John says you have family awaiting your return." He tapped a finger against his chin, ignoring John, who was making faces at him. "I have to wonder how you came to be in the Tower of London, alone and unescorted?"

She looked at John. "Didn't you tell him?"

He fidgeted. "A bit. 'Tis your story to tell. Robert is a bothersome lad, but he has a good ear. He will keep your secrets."

She looked at Robert, who pressed a hand to his heart.

Anna rolled her eyes. These two together were going to be more trouble than a pool full of alligators. "Okay. Here goes." She sat upright in the chair, afraid to wrinkle the dress. Anna told Robert the same story she'd told John. This time, though, she told them the rest of the story. The part she left out before.

"I am an only child. My mother died after a long illness when I was eighteen. I was away at college... university. In my first semester, I had to drop out to take care of my dad. He had a stroke when my mother died."

She sniffed but did not cry. A cup was thrust into her hands, and she gave John a grateful smile as she took a sip.

"Water. You remembered."

Robert looked horrified. "Why did you not give the lass wine?"

"She prefers water." He looked at his brother and smirked. "'Tis what she prefers, and she shall have what she desires."

"So I found a full-time job. But it still wasn't enough. So I also found two part-time jobs to help pay for the facility." She saw the look on their faces and clarified: "My father was in the beginning stages of Alzheimer's. It's where you start to forget things and no longer recognize those you love. A stroke is when you lose control of part of your body. My dad can no longer move the left side of his body, and requires someone to watch over him day and night. There are places to help with his care. But they cost a great deal of money."

"You worked? For money?" They both looked extremely interested. Feeling self-conscious, she continued.

"Yes. For forty hours a week I worked as an

assistant." She looked at the blank looks on their faces and added, "It's where someone tells you they need things done and you do them. So the full-time job I worked Monday through Friday, all day. In the evenings I worked in a small shop, and on the weekends I worked as a waitress in a diner. It's like the tavern we stopped at. We take people's orders and bring them food."

"A serving wench?" Robert pursed his lips.

"No. There are no serving wenches anymore." She paused. "Well, there are, but if they're like the ones I've seen so far, we call them hookers."

Her throat was dry from talking so much. She was used to sitting on the sidelines, not being the center of attention. It was discomforting having two men such as the Thornton brothers turning their full attention on her. But she was almost through with her story, and she had to get it all out before she lost her nerve.

"So you can understand why I have to get back. The place where my father stays, I have paid for this month and the next, but after that, if there is no money, they will make him leave and he will have nowhere to go. Then they put you in a place the state pays for, and the one near our town is a terrible, dreadful place. I must go home."

"I'm sorry you lost your family," John said. Robert looked at John, who nodded. "We may know someone who can help you."

"The Melinda you heard us talking about when you

came in has two sisters," Robert said. "I am not certain, but I believe they may also come from the future. 'Tis something about their speech, they use the same words you do. Such as *whatever*. A most useful word for many occasions."

Robert held his hands up.

"Do not get excited. We do not know if they can travel forward to their own time. But we will find out. Our brother Henry is married to the third sister, Charlotte. He is on his way and should be here on the morrow. We will ask."

She couldn't help it—the excitement filled her entire being. A possible way to go home. And the chance to talk to others who had traveled through time. To find out how and what their experience was. And if they could go back, had they all stayed of their own free will? Was it for the men they married?

The three of them stayed up late talking. The deep voices were comforting, lulling her into a state somewhere between dreaming and wakefulness. Anna couldn't stop yawning, and thought she'd close her eyes just for a moment.

"I fear I care for an witless woman." John lifted Anna out of the chair to carry her upstairs.

"If her story is true, she is not witless. You could marry her."

"You know why I cannot. Her life would always be in danger." John opened the door to the chamber and laid her on the bed.

"Have you shared a bed with her?"

His brother looked furious, and John tried not to laugh.

"The other chambers are in disrepair. I have behaved honorably and slept with the horses."

"'Tis a clear night. The other chambers will do. Edward is sending his mason and men. Henry will be here in the morning. You must take care with her. Though she is not noble, she is a lady."

John rolled his eyes. "Cease with your witless babbling. I would not take advantage of her."

Robert clapped him on the shoulder. "You do more than care for her. You love her. When will you see it yourself?"

Chapter Twenty

Anna was walking around Blackmoor with John while Robert slept in.

"Riders approach."

"Come. We'll go up on the battlements for a better look."

She followed John. It was a long way down. With a hand up to shade her eyes, she wished for sunglasses. They were around in some form in ancient China and Rome. Imagine gems for sunnies. If she was stuck here maybe she could create sunglasses for the rich. It wasn't like she could rely on John to support her. Anna would have to find a way to make a living and a place to live.

"Wow. That's a lot of people."

The man with gorgeous blonde hair she'd recognize anywhere waved to them. A beautiful blonde beside him. Behind him walked men and women. There were men who looked like soldiers and wagons bursting with stuff. In one of the wagons, she spied pigs and chickens.

"He looks like you. Which brother is it?"

John's words were gruff. "Henry has grown to a man. I have missed so much time."

Anna knew the feeling all too well. As the group entered the courtyard, the level of noise rose to a crescendo. The blonde man dismounted from his horse, and helped a striking woman do the same. She was tall and thin, blonde, and looked like Barbie come to life. Anna was completely intimidated.

"I should have known you were still alive. The bandit of the wood. Well done." Henry hugged John. His voice was rough. Anna stood close enough to hear him say, "You should have told us you were alive. I have missed you every day for the past ten years."

"I could not. Our family was dishonored. The loss of our lands, titles, gold. So much lost because of a jealous girl. If Letitia had kept quiet, the king would not have turned his wrath on the Thorntons. There is a large price on my head. You should not have come."

"Our father would have been gladdened to know you were alive." Henry released John and stood back, looking at Blackmoor. "Robert let it fall to ruin. Too busy drinking and whoring."

"I heard that, whelp." Robert clapped Henry on the shoulder.

John looked a bit overwhelmed. "I'm grateful you're here, Henry. But we are bound to attract undue attention."

"Our people are loyal. Others in the surrounding countryside are loyal to the Thorntons."

Robert rocked back on his heels. "And many others to the bandit of the wood. News has traveled fast. Everyone knows 'twas you. Do not worry, brother. None will betray us."

John grimaced. "Betrayal comes when we least expect it."

"What an awful thing to say." Anna wished she could take it back. Now everyone was looking at her.

Henry's mouth twitched. She blushed where she stood. "You have obviously made her miserable with your foul moods." He made her a little bow. "I am the most charming and handsome brother. Henry Thornton, at your service." He pulled the gorgeous woman forward, interrupting her conversation with a group of women.

"My wife, Charlotte."

Anna smiled, feeling like the frumpy girl facing the head cheerleader. The woman pulled her into a hug.

"I'm so happy to meet you." She looked to the men. "What have y'all been doing? Hell's bells. This place looks like it was used for target practice."

Anna blinked up at the tall Amazon goddess. Charlotte was Southern. As in Southern United States of

America. It was true. Another time traveler.

Charlotte winked. "It's a beautiful day. Let's go for a walk and leave the men to unload the wagons."

She took Anna's hand, pulling her toward a mass of weeds that at one point she supposed might have been a garden.

"Y'all get this mess taken care of. Anna and I have womanly things to discuss."

"Best not to argue with her," Henry said to his brothers. Anna giggled as they walked away.

"Lucy's going to be so jealous, she hasn't met John yet." Charlotte's eyes sparkled. She was as nice as she was pretty. The tension left Anna's shoulders and neck. "Talk about major scoop. Wait until they hear John has a girlfriend."

Anna blinked. "I'm not his girlfriend. When I landed in the past and helped him escape, I thought I was in the middle of a movie."

Charlotte laughed. "Oh, honey, we all had that feeling."

"It's true, then?" Where else would she have learned to talk like she did but the future?

"What?" Charlotte gazed up at her, a look of such feigned innocence that Anna knew without a doubt she too was from the future.

"Robert and John said they thought so. Tell me I'm right."

Charlotte shot her a wary look. "What exactly do you think you're right about?"

Anna huffed. She wanted to play it like this, huh? Fine. "Pizza. Hot showers. *The Walking Dead*. Chris Hemsworth. Bikinis. Cell phones. Shall I go on?"

Charlotte groaned. "Chocolate, Pepsi, and Pop-Tarts." She pulled Anna to the corner of the wall where no one could sneak up on them. "Tell me what I've missed on *The Walking Dead*. My oh my, that Daryl Dixon."

"I don't know where to start. I'm still trying to get my mind right. Someone like me. Another time traveler."

"Oh my goodness, I can't believe I'm talking to someone from my own time. Well, other than my sisters."

"Where are you from?"

"North Carolina. Holden Beach. You?"

"Venice, Florida. I miss the beach."

"You'll come visit. If I didn't invite you, Melinda and Lucy might chop off my head. Melinda has a new baby. Lucy and William are dealing with a small skirmish, so they couldn't come either, but you'll meet them all. Wait until you see the ocean. The beach and the water aren't anything like the Gulf of Mexico, but the smell is the same. Well, except for the sunscreen. I miss the smell of coconut oil."

The dreamy look on Charlotte's face was probably the same look on her own face.

"Me too. And music."

"Books."

"Movies."

Charlotte sighed. "Tell me how it happened to you."

"It all began when I found out I was taking my first vacation in five years. Two whole weeks in England. I landed in London..."

She and Charlotte found a stone bench partially buried in the weeds. They pulled enough away to sit. They both leaned against the wall, faces tilted up to the sun. It was so nice to talk to someone from her own time.

Charlotte had been here the least amount of time. Anna couldn't believe Charlotte's sister, Lucy, had been in the past over twenty years. From everything she told her, Charlotte's sisters sounded like the kinds of friends Anna wished she'd had. But when you dropped out of college and worked three jobs, you didn't have time to make friends with anyone, or date, or do much of anything.

"I can't believe you figured out your sisters went back in time. You planned your own trip back in time. I wish I would've paid more attention in history class."

"I know, right? It's not like any of us thought we would ever need to apply the knowledge in a real-life situation." Charlotte turned serious. "I've seen the way John looks at you. You say he's not your boyfriend, but I can tell he cares for you. And you seem to care for him. Am I totally off base?"

"I can't care for him. I have to get home." And now, Charlotte had provided the small sliver of hope Anna needed. She had been ready to give up. Now maybe she could get back, but she had to be in the tower when she tried.

For the first time since her mom died, Anna felt something wet on her cheek. She touched a finger to her face. Tears.

"Oh, sweetie, let it all out." Charlotte pulled her close, hugging her. Anna couldn't remember the last time anyone touched her with a comforting touch. To feel close with another human being without them wanting anything from you or expecting anything—it was almost more than she could bear.

John had been kind to her and touched her, but this was different. It was like Charlotte could be the sister she never had, but had always yearned for. She sobbed, letting the tears run down her face and puddle by her feet.

It seemed like hours had passed when Anna finally wiped her eyes.

"I'm such an ugly crier. And I've ruined your dress."

"Don't worry about it, sweetie. We've all had that moment when we realize we're here for good. I'm so very sorry. I cannot imagine what you're going through. My sisters were already here and I didn't have anyone left to go back to."

Anna sniffed. "I'm so worried about my dad. But in some small way it's almost a relief. If I can't get back then I know it isn't my fault. Part of me thought about staying here."

She hesitated. "Not that I thought I would be with John. But in the time I've been here, I've grown to love this time. Things are harder, yet easier."

Charlotte took her hand. "I know, right? I think about someone being flung back in time and not being able to acclimate. I guess they wouldn't survive. If we all did it, I wonder how many others have traveled through time? And did anyone from the past go forward?"

"There's something to be said for being adaptable. Knowing I'm almost certainly stuck here instead of thinking I could go back and didn't try hard enough, it makes the pain a little bit easier to bear. I just wish I could get a message to my dad." She pursed her lips. "But from what you told me, it doesn't matter anyway. You didn't even get the message your sisters left."

"I have been looking for you, wife." Henry stood in front of them, sweaty and disheveled. He saw Anna's face. His eyes widened. "Is my wife making you cry?"

Charlotte smacked him on the arm. "We were having

a girl talk. Anna's fine."

And the funny thing was, Charlotte was right. She was fine. No matter what happened from this day forward, she was at peace. She would try one last time at the tower, and if it didn't work, she would build a life here. Based on what Charlotte told her, there was a moment when each of them thought they could go back but they chose not to, so they didn't know if they actually could. And if they did, there was no certainty they'd end up back in their own time.

It was enough to give her a migraine. Anna would always be sad about never saying goodbye to her dad, not being there to pay for his care. But knowing she couldn't do anything about it and was stuck across an ocean of time made it just the tiniest bit easier to accept. If, by a miracle, she did go back, well, she'd deal with her broken heart then.

Now if she could only figure out if John liked her the tiniest bit.

Chapter Twenty-One

The days passed quickly. Each day Anna and Charlotte explored the tattered remains of Blackmoor Castle, a large key ring in hand. Emory handed over the keys and said he was going to stay with his sister in the village. He couldn't stand all the racket and chaos after being alone at the castle for so long.

John and Henry, along with the rest of the men, were busy making repairs. John grumbled it would be a waste, since he'd die soon enough. Anna caught him looking over the work a few times, a smile on his face.

He was afraid. That was why he acted like they shouldn't bother with repairs. He didn't want to lose his home twice. So she didn't say too much about the work or the future as they waited for John's oldest brother, Edward, to send his mason and more men. They would need to accomplish a great deal of work in order for the place to be habitable by winter.

Winter. It was the first time she'd actually thought about a future here. Now was not the time, not when there was the tiniest sliver of hope she might be able to get back to her dad and her own time. She felt the passage of time. Soon she would have to insist it was time for her to leave.

"Hey, look what I found." Charlotte wiped a smudge of dirt off her cheek as she poked her head out of a door at the end of the corridor.

Anna pointed. "You have cobwebs in your hair."

Charlotte shrieked and brushed it away. She peered at Anna. "I'm afraid you have one on your shoulder and on your back. Turn around."

At least Anna didn't shriek, though she might have jumped. Just a little. She turned so Charlotte could wipe the cobweb and who knows what else off her dress.

"Thank you again for the dress. It's nice to have two so I can rotate them."

"Don't mention it. I'm having a seamstress come next week. You need more to wear. If I left it to John, you'd still be walking around in your grubby jeans. Men. Clueless."

"One of the women threw my jeans and t-shirt in the fire. I know they were absolutely disgusting...do you think it will harm my chances to go back?"

Charlotte chewed her bottom lip. "My sisters and I

talked a lot about how we traveled through time. We don't think you have to be wearing what you arrived in." She patted her arm. "It's for the best. Lucy was almost burned as a witch. Jeans are bad."

"Don't you miss wearing jeans?"

"All the time. And shorts and flip-flops. You?"

"I do, though it certainly is easy wearing a dress like this." Anna looked down at the long dress with a simple apron over it. "I didn't think pockets had been invented yet."

Charlotte winked. "My sisters and I put them in all of our dresses. I don't know how anyone survives without pockets."

They looked over the room they'd unlocked. It was crammed floor to ceiling with furniture and bedding and other assorted bits and pieces. Guess Robert and Henry didn't take everything with them. Talk about a daunting task. Anna was glad Charlotte was here to help her.

"All righty then, let's start by pulling everything out into the hallway so we can see what we've got." Charlotte dusted her hands off and slid what looked like a piece of a bed out of the room. "Can you imagine trying to move all this stuff if the floors were carpeted?"

"No way. I love hardwood and tile floors. You can move most furniture by yourself." Anna held up what must've been bedding at some point but looked as if the rats and mice had had a field day over the years. "I'm thinking rag pile for these."

"Ugh. Absolutely. Don't worry; Henry and I brought plenty of bedding, pillows, and other odds and ends."

"It's so nice to have someone to talk to...you know, from our own time." Anna was prevented from saying more as a small girl and boy skidded to a stop in front of them.

"My lord says we're to come and help you, lady."

"Fetch buckets with water and soap. Then wipe down all the furniture." Charlotte barked out orders, and Anna was impressed. She looked like such a sweet thing, but she probably could command her husband's guards with a single glare. Anna felt a tiny twinge of jealousy. What she wouldn't give to have that confidence and boldness.

As if Charlotte knew what she was thinking, she nudged Anna with an elbow. "They need a firm hand and expect to be ordered about. Try it." She grinned. "Once you get used to it, you'll find the power quite heady stuff."

"I believe you. I've seen the crew you put to work scouring the hall and kitchen."

"Don't worry, Anna. We'll have this place gleaming in no time." Charlotte looked up at the roof. "That's assuming there aren't any other holes in the roof and it doesn't rain and ruin all our hard work."

The day flew by as they talked of their old lives. What they missed, the things they had been glad to leave behind.

"...at first I couldn't live without my phone and

checking in on social media. Even when I traveled I was always plugged in. Totally addicted. But now, I like the fact I live my life and everyone doesn't have to know what I'm doing every moment of the day. And I don't need to know what they're doing every moment either."

Charlotte sat on a chair they'd pulled from the room and wiped her brow. She'd sent the kids down for clean water.

"There are people at Falconburg who have been there their entire lives. It certainly changes your perspective, doesn't it?"

"You're not kidding. I'm glad I have a good sense of direction. Imagine being here without the maps app on your phone."

Charlotte burst out laughing. "We Merriweather sisters are known for one thing above all others...we're all dreadful with directions."

They both laughed. Anna peeked up at her new friend.

"Is this what it would be like to have a sister?"

Charlotte hugged her. "Absolutely. I want you to know, you are officially an honorary Merriweather. And the Merriweather sisters stick together. No matter what."

Charlotte sat back and took a sip of wine. When their stomachs started to growl, she'd sent one of the girls down to bring up food and drink.

"Now you have three sisters, Anna." She wiped a tear

from the corner of her eye. "Look what you've done; you've made me cry."

Anna half laughed, half sobbed as she too wiped her eyes. "When I go back to my own time, I'll never forget you."

Charlotte patted her arm. "Oh, sweetie. I hope you can get back. Though a part of me wishes you would stay. I think you're good for John, and I can see how much you care for each other."

"I do. A great deal."

"Has the work reduced both of you to weeping?" John stood there, hands on his hips.

Anna winced. Please don't let him have heard what she said.

"No. We were just talking about our families," Anna said as she and Charlotte shared a look. Her heart skipped a beat. It was a look she had seen many times over the years, but never one she'd shared with anyone. It was a look between family that said, *I'm here, sis. I've got your back, no matter what.*

Chapter Twenty-Two

Three days later, Anna stood in the courtyard saying goodbye to Charlotte.

"Thank you so much for all you've done. I won't forget it."

Charlotte whispered in her ear, "If it's what you truly want, I hope you can go back. But if you can't, know that you have sisters here who care about you." She leaned back and waggled her eyebrows. "Not to mention that gorgeous hunk of a man who is totally smitten with you."

Henry helped Charlotte onto the horse, and then pulled Anna into a hug. "Take care of my brother."

"Thank you again for everything."

There was a low stone wall nearby that would be the perfect vantage point for watching them leave. As Anna made her way over to the wall, she couldn't help but overhear John talking to Henry.

"...I care not if she stays or goes back to her own time. Every moment she is by my side, I am responsible for her. Nay, Henry. I do not want her here."

She pressed a fist against her mouth, trying to hold in the gasp. Why didn't people realize how deeply words could cut? While she knew she shouldn't have been listening to their conversation, she heard what John said to Henry. He didn't want her here and didn't care for her.

Somehow she managed to sit next to him on the wall as they watched Henry and Charlotte depart, the empty wagons rumbling in a line behind them. A large number of men had stayed behind and would remain until Edward's men arrived. It seemed quiet after the busy comings and goings of the past week. Henry left Sara, two of the girls, and two boys to help out with whatever needed to be done. Thank goodness for Sara. The woman was a terrific cook.

Her voice stuck in her throat. Anna coughed. "I'm going to spend the afternoon pulling weeds in the garden. It's a beautiful day and I want to finish before it rains again."

"I will see you for supper." He nodded absently as he made his way to the stables.

No he wouldn't. Anna planned to be long gone by then.

It was time. Five weeks. In three more there would be no more money for her dad's care. She was out of time. The economy was tough. By now, she'd certainly been fired from all three of her jobs. The full-time job would be the hardest loss. It paid the most and offered modest benefits. The two part-time jobs would sting. If she made it back, she would be faced with being unemployed and homeless.

By now Anna figured the landlord had sold her stuff. The guy managed the building for his father. In his twenties, he was more concerned with partying than doing anything for the tenants. She'd called numerous times to get the air conditioning fixed or have the place sprayed for roaches. And in Florida they grew to the size of toy cars. The guy always had an excuse. But let a tenant be late on the rent...the second time it happened, you found yourself evicted.

Yep, Anna was sure he'd sold her stuff. So if she did make it back, she would be broke and homeless, but at least she'd have her dad. Somehow she'd find more work and keep paying the fees. Maybe she could clean the facility or do other work there to keep him there until she found something. He was her father; she'd do anything for him.

How different might her life have been if she'd been able to stay in college? Get her degree and a better-paying job? Anna would never know.

To think she'd actually considered staying here with John.

In high school she'd had boyfriends but no one serious. There was one guy that summer. Then in college, it was only one semester and she hadn't met anyone she really liked. The years passed, and with working three jobs she didn't have time for friends, let alone boyfriends. Now at the ripe old age of twenty-three, she wondered if she would end up alone for the rest of her life.

She ripped up another handful of weeds and flung them to the side. So what if she was plain? She wasn't ugly or hard to get along with. The mousy girl never got the Hollywood hunk...except in the movies. It had been ridiculous of her to think John would ever want her. When she made it back home, Anna would make an effort to find a guy who was right for her. Who didn't care what she looked like on the outside. The inside was all they'd have when they were old and wrinkled.

Time to take control of her life. She was done waiting for John to decide when the right time was to take her back to the tower. He had no intention of taking her back. She would feel the same way, but couldn't he have provided her with a horse or a man to accompany her?

Fine. He thought she was such a bother, she would go alone. He wouldn't even notice. John and Robert were occupied with figuring out how to get the king to pardon him. Not a soul would notice if she left.

Wiping dust and grass from her skirts, Anna felt a little better. Being in limbo took a lot of energy. Now she had a plan. She made her way through the hall, stopping by a small room that was really more of an alcove. Three of the boys had made a makeshift chamber with a pallet on the floor and a chair to throw clothes over.

The laundry was done, so she knew she would find something clean. With a peek over her shoulder to make sure no one was watching, Anna took a tunic and hose from one of the boys Henry left behind. He was just about her height. John and his brothers were all over six feet tall, so she'd be swimming in their hose.

She rolled the clothing and tucked it under her arm. Back in her chamber, she quickly washed and took the cloth covering the pillow. It would do as a makeshift bag. John had given her a small dagger to keep in her boot. Hopefully she'd only use it to eat. A quick look out the window to see the men and boys practicing swordplay in the lists. By now, preparations would be underway for tonight's meal. It was the perfect time to go.

Hurt feelings bubbled up. No, she wouldn't cry. This was for the best. Why stay where you weren't wanted?

Knowing he didn't want her, didn't care for her, would make it much easier to go back. In time she would forget him. He would become a distant memory. Fading to a dream over the years...at least, that was what she kept telling herself.

With a peek down the hallway, Anna crossed to the chamber where John was sleeping. She'd liked sleeping curled up next to him on the journey here. In this day and age it was inappropriate, even though nothing had happened. She rummaged through a small trunk at the foot of the bed. Something clinked. She came up with a heavy bag. Opening it, she saw the gold within. She'd never even stolen a pack of gum. Anna felt horribly guilty, but she saw no other way. There were a lot of coins in the bag. A big handful should be plenty. The rest she put back. She had to have some way to purchase food and shelter on the way back to London. If it worked, if she could travel back through time, there was no way she could ever repay John.

If she found herself stuck in the past, it likely wouldn't matter either, as she would be imprisoned in the tower for helping him escape in the first place. And then she would definitely need the money to pay for her accommodations. There wasn't any paper to leave him a note, so she had to hope he would understand when he found the gold missing.

Anna stopped in the kitchens. "I know we'll be eating in a few hours, but I missed dinner."

One of the girls pointed to bread cooling on the stone. The rest were too busy going about their chores to pay her any attention. She packed up food for a week and took an empty ceramic jug. On her way out, she'd fill it with water from the well.

Outside, she passed the girl who'd helped her dress that morning.

"Tell John my head aches. I will eat in my room and go to bed early."

"Shall I bring you a bit of ale and bread, mistress?"

"No. I just need to sleep and I'll be right as rain on the morrow."

"As you will."

Anna bypassed the lists and made her way to the ruined chapel. She sat on a slab of stone and listened. John sounded happier and younger after spending time with his brothers. She could hear him jesting and cursing with the men as they hacked away at each other.

How she wished she'd had brothers and sisters. Not only for the company. But to know you weren't alone in the world. That they could help take care of her dad if she couldn't return. The thought of being stuck here for the rest of her life made Anna want to cry. And it made her cry to think of leaving. No, she had to believe Charlotte.

It took her a moment to realize she wasn't hearing the sound of ringing steel or the men's voices. Risking a peek around the doorway, she exhaled. All clear. She filled the bottle with water from the well and, keeping to the wall, made her way out of the gate.

The men Henry had brought were already inside. Over the past few days she'd noticed the man guarding the gate always fell asleep when he was supposed to be on duty. Seemed like eating made him sleepy. She wasn't complaining; it made her task of leaving undetected much easier. She slipped out of the gates and ran across open ground, only slowing her pace slightly to make sure she was staying on the path. The last thing she needed was to end up stuck in a bog or to fall off a cliff and die before she made it back to London. She'd seriously considered stealing a horse, but not being confident in her abilities to care for the animal, she decided against it. The trip would take so much longer. She hoped she'd find someone with a wagon who would be going the same direction and she could catch a ride.

Anna knew others had difficulties with directions. She'd overheard people when she worked in the diner. Someone up above had seen fit to give her a strong sense of direction. If she'd been to a place once, she always remembered how to get back.

Coming to a small wood, she stopped inside the tree line, panting, doubled over, hands on her knees. Once she caught her breath, Anna sat down with her back against the rough bark.

She never got lost. So how had she ended up lost in

the Tower of London? A snort escaped. "Secret passages don't count. Not like you'd been in one before.

"Still, I should have found my way easily enough when I made it back outside."

Great. Now she was arguing with herself. Out loud.

Anna rolled her eyes like an annoyed teenager. She recapped the bottle and stood. Time to get going and put as much distance between she and Blackmoor as possible before dark.

Chapter Twenty-Three

As Anna picked her way across the moors, she had plenty of time to think about how she'd ended up in the past. She replayed the conversation she had with Charlotte. They both experienced being caught in a thunderstorm. What else was similar?

She thought back to her visit to the tower. The locket. It was definitely old. She'd run her finger across the rough edge where half the picture was missing. And then she'd fallen, skinning her palm on the rough stone. The blood on her palm was on the same hand in which she held the locket. That was when the horrible ringing noise filled her head. The bright, brilliant blue light filled the room, pulsing around her and penetrating and every cell of her body.

Here was a problem. While she could re-create the

blood by scraping her hand on stone, and she could wait until a storm blew in. What did she do about the locket? It was important from what Charlotte told Anna of her own experiences. John hadn't given her any such piece of jewelry, and it wasn't like she would have enough money left to buy one by the time she reached London. Who was the man in the portrait? Based on Charlotte's experience, it had to be John. She'd looked through the trunk, and there was no such locket. Could it still be in his cell at the tower?

Anna stretched out on a flat stone next to a brook, greedily drinking water while she thought about her chances. For the life of her, she couldn't remember if she still had the locket in her hand when she appeared in the past or had dropped it when the blue lightning flashed around her. The biggest unknown was: how important was the jewelry? Guess she'd find out soon enough. Anna looked to the south. Okay, not soon. It would take her almost three weeks if she had to walk the entire way to London. Not acceptable. She needed to be home sooner, and who knew how long she'd have to wait for a storm and to sneak into the tower? Though she'd bet it was much easier to sneak in than out.

Thankful she was used to being on her feet for long hours working at the diner, Anna was happy to stop for the night. She found some scrubby trees and rocks. Curling up under the trees, she listened. Nothing but the wind. She draped a cloak over her. His cloak. While she hadn't taken his clothes, she did swipe the cloak. It was big and warm, and she thought it could serve as a blanket or a pillow or whatever else she might need.

The food would last a week, so whenever she saw a home, she could buy food as John had. The villagers could be suspicious, and she stood out. They knew she was different. At least now she was dressed appropriately, wearing one of the dresses. The other dress and tunic and hose were packed with her food supplies. Why hadn't she thought to bring anything to start a fire? Matches. That was another thing that would have come in handy.

"Look at it this way, it could be winter and then you'd freeze your butt off. At least it isn't cold."

Her voice sounded loud in the silence. Anna wrapped the cloak tight and curled into a ball. It was different sleeping out on the ground when she'd traveled with John. They'd been together, had each other's back. Now she was alone and it was a lot scarier.

A small snort escaped as she remembered when she was a little girl and had desperately wanted to join the Girl Scouts. It had been all fun and games until it was time for the camping trip. Not only had it rained, but one of the girls woke up to find a small black snake curled up at the foot of her sleeping bag. It was on the outside, but still, all the girls went shrieking out of the tent.

Then they heard a hissing noise and two red eyes

glowed in the beam of the troop leader's flashlight. It was an alligator walking across the campsite. He ambled along, tail swinging back and forth. They all slept in the cars. After that, Anna swore she would never go camping again.

Now her idea of camping was a motel without a hair dryer. And yet here she was. At least here in England she wouldn't have to worry about alligators or snakes.

No, dummy, but you're going to have to worry about bandits slitting your throat while you sleep.

Great. She certainly didn't need the voice in her head coming up with all kinds of ghastly scenarios while she tried to fall asleep.

Where was Anna? John had been so busy with the repairs, he couldn't remember the last time he saw her. He stopped one of the wenches from the village who had come to see the men.

"Have you seen Mistress Waters?"

The woman pushed her shoulders back, showing off her breasts. She leaned close. "Nay, my lord. 'Tis her womanly time of the month. She will be spending the next sen'night in her chamber."

He thanked her and went about his business. But when she did not appear after a sen'night, John grew worried.

He asked every man, woman, and child, and none had seen her. One of the girls spoke up.

"I saw Mistress Waters the day Lord Ravenskirk left."

"You are certain?"

"Aye, my lord."

He knew Anna did not depart with Henry and Charlotte—they sat together as his brother left. Where the bloody hell was she?

As he was poking his head into the chapel, the wench from the village ran, skirts flying around her legs.

"The king's men, three villages over." She ground out the words, staring at a spot over his shoulder.

"Tell me, woman."

The woman blubbered. "I wanted ye for myself. Thought if I got rid of her, you would take me to your bed. I watched her leave Blackmoor the day your brother and his lady left."

"A sen'night. She's been gone a bloody sen'night?" John bellowed. "Damnation. Saddle my horse."

Fear clawed at his insides. He knew where she was going. The daft woman was going back to the tower. To go home to her own time. If, by the fates, she made it to London, the guards would throw her in a cell after they used her ill. He cursed in three languages as he galloped through the gates.

Chapter Twenty-Four

The days quickly turned routine. Anna wished for a car. Wished for a hotel and a hot shower. And, most of all, wondered why John had not come after her. Wasn't he supposed to be a knight? More like a dark, fallen knight. He knew how important going home was to her. He could have at least sent someone to take her as far as London. But no one appeared. As the days passed, she too passed, from sadness to anger.

This morning she'd taken the time to wash. She debated forever then undressed and washed the chemise as best she could. Her best dress she would save until she was almost to London. After dressing in tunic and hose, she laid the wet garments over the rocks to dry. As she sat in the sun, warmth put her to sleep.

When she woke, Anna guessed it must be around

lunchtime. The rocks were too exposed. She needed to find somewhere safe to sleep tonight. Not by water; too many people or animals would pass by. A quick bite and then she packed up her dry clothes and trudged along the path. Maybe a few more hours and she would stop for the night.

How dare he not help her after she had freed him? The risk she had taken. Had it meant nothing? Was he so self-absorbed all he could think about was himself? Anna ranted and raved until she was exhausted. Deep down, she knew he was a good man. But it certainly made her feel better to scream and yell and say all kinds of hateful things about the man.

As she was stomping about, Anna lost her footing and fell into a huge mud puddle. As she struggled, the muck pulled at her clothes, pulling her deeper. Oh hell, she must be in a bog. She scrabbled for a branch to pull herself out. There wasn't even a bush nearby. Her fingers touched mud but couldn't find anything to pull herself out. Panic made her kick and scream, only making things worse.

Was she going to die out here all alone? The thought of drowning by mud made her feel dizzy.

"No! You will not faint. You will stay calm and figure out a way out of this."

She screamed, hoping someone would hear her. Screamed until she was hoarse and could only manage a croak. As night fell, Anna was up to her waist in the bog.

If someone didn't find her within the next day or two, she would slowly sink until she drowned. No one would ever know what happened to her.

At least the madwoman had the wits to stay on the path. The moors could be dangerous to those unfamiliar with them. She was easy to track. John made good time on horseback. Why hadn't the bloody woman stolen a horse? Likely it had not occurred to her, as she did not ride in her own time. Why would she leave without telling him?

Terrible thoughts filled his mind. Had Denby or one of his men promised her gold or a way to get back to her own time in return for betraying him?

He dismounted to examine her tracks. The king's men were near, but he would not believe her capable of betrayal. She was too full of goodness. He snorted. Though she had taken the stable boys tunic and hose. And stolen a bit of his gold. Why hadn't she taken the bag?

It looked as though she had taken only what she needed for her travels. He would've gladly given her all she asked. He stopped. John had been so consumed with his own problems he had not taken the time to understand what it must mean to be lost in time.

John had made the choice not to tell his brothers he was alive. Anna had a sick father who depended upon her to see to his well-being. Would he not have done the same in her situation?

He tracked her, aware of spending too much time with his own thoughts. Was it possible she'd heard him talking to Henry? He had been in a foul temper and did not mean what he said. He did not wish she had never come. Did not wish her to go.

Nay. He cared for her a great deal, in truth. The thought filled him with fear. Of what would happen if he lost her. If she stayed by his side when the king's men came for him. For them both. 'Twas only a matter of time until they found him and took him back to answer for his crime all those years ago. Now he was known as John Thornton and the bandit, he had many more crimes to answer for.

Her tracks had taken her in a circle as she tried to avoid some of the more treacherous areas. She was being careful and missed some of the less-used paths that would have taken her in a more direct route through the moors. Did she realize she was not moving forward but in circles?

'Twas the middle of the third day when he saw something ahead. Sunlight turned the mud to gold. John thought his heart would cease beating.

"Anna!"

He heard nothing and tried again. "I'm coming, love. Hold fast."

As he strained to listen, he swore he heard her voice, hoarse and feeble, carried on the wind to him.

"I'm drowning."

John jumped from the horse as the final bit of stone around his heart crumbled to dust. She was trapped in a bog up to her breasts.

"I don't want to die."

"You will not die. I will not allow you to leave me." John uncoiled the rope he had brought with him. "You must not thrash about. Take the rope and wrap it around your waist tightly."

Her eyes were wild, her face pale. John would never forgive himself if he lost her.

"I'm so tired. I don't think I can do it."

"You must."

Her hands shook as she took the rope and pulled it into the muck.

"I know 'tis hard, but do not struggle." John took the other end and tied it to the saddle. He came back, kneeling at the edge.

"Try to lie back and let your body float upward."

"The mud is too thick. It will not work."

He looked into her eyes, willing her to see how much he cared.

"Slow your breathing. Look at me, Anna. Nowhere

else. Look to me." Once he saw she had calmed a bit, he said, "Do you know how to swim?"

"Of course. I grew up in Florida, on the beach."

"Good. You must think of the bog as the ocean. Lie back and let it lift you up. It will take time, but it will work."

He did not voice his worry. That he could not free her. He could not risk going back for help. There wasn't enough time. If he left her much longer, the bog would take her. 'Twas an awful way to die.

The waiting was agony. John told her of his time in the wood. Anything to pass the time. Told her how he became the outlaw.

"...so when Robin died, I became the bandit of the wood. He had seen to it his reputation spread across the realm, and people were afraid to enter the wood."

"All so he could provide a home for people?"

"That is why we took nobles for ransom and their gold. They have plenty to spare. People are hungry. They have been burned out of their villages, and they come to the woods seeking shelter."

"Now that the king knows, will you have to pay for the crimes of being the bandit too?"

"Most likely. We shall worry about it when the time comes. My brothers are wealthy, and so are James and William. Together they are formidable. I did not want to accept their aid, but it appears I have no choice."

He could see her body lifting. He would not wait any

longer.

"I want you to hold on to the rope. Do not struggle."

"I have faith in you."

And with that simple declaration, all the reasons why he could not care for her drifted away like dust on the wind. He would love her for as long as he had left. And trust his brothers to protect her if the time came and he was sentenced to death.

He slowly urged the horse forward. The rope tightened and he heard the sounds of the bog trying to hold on to Anna. He urged the horse forward, and with a great sucking sound she was free.

John removed the rope from her. "Do not ever scare me like that again."

He crushed her to him, heedless of the mud and smell. Lowered his lips to hers. Her lips were soft as the softest silk. Warm. The rest of her was cold. She made a sound in the back of her throat. Her arms came around his neck. Her lips parted and he lost himself in the taste of her. The feel of her against him. When they broke apart, she was breathing heavily, her voice shaking.

"I'm warm now."

He threw back his head and laughed. Gave thanks he'd found her in time.

"Let's go home."

Chapter Twenty-Five

John led her to a nearby stream, turning his back while she removed the garments.

"I think I'm going to be brown forever."

"In time the color will fade from your skin. There is a woman at the castle who has herbs you can add to the bath to remove the coloring."

He heard splashing. John had to strain to hear the words.

"I'm getting dressed. Don't look."

He heard a rustling noise and kept his eyes averted, though he was most curious.

As she fell asleep that night, Anna cried and moaned in her sleep. John stroked her hair, comforting her as he would a spooked horse.

He was unused to spending so much time with a

woman. So many years he'd visited a wench to satisfy his needs but never wanted to have speech with them. Never cared what they thought. With Anna, he wanted to know every thought she had.

The next morning, she was quiet, sitting stiffly in the saddle in front of him. The entire day she said less than a handful of words.

Would she not speak the entire way back to Blackmoor? Most women would have babbled incessantly. John never had to work to get a woman to talk. Anna said not a word.

On the third day of travel, John decided he'd had enough of her silence. They sat by the fire.

"I know you do not care for wine, but you must not take a chill after being in the bog for so long."

She wrinkled her nose but drank it anyway. They ate a simple meal. She had two more cups of wine and still she did not speak.

Anna dropped the cup to the ground. "I'm going to the ladies' room. I'll be back in a few minutes."

"Ladies' room?"

She made a face at him. "You know."

He was perplexed for a moment then laughed. Seeing the displeasure on her face, he shut his mouth with a snap. He held out his hands in front of him.

"I meant no offense."

John heard her stomping through the brush. If the king's men had been near, they would have heard her.

She swayed a bit as she came to a stop in front of him. Anna leaned down and poked him in the chest.

"I heard what you said to Henry." She wobbled so he pulled her down beside him, afraid she would fall over. She slapped his hand away.

"Don't touch me. You said you didn't care if I stayed or went back to my own time. That you are tired of me being your responsibility." She belched. "You don't want me here. So why are you taking me back? I would've made it to London eventually."

"You would? Walking in circles? Would that be before or after you drowned in the bog?"

"Don't be mean to me. I don't know why I even care. Someone as sexy and good-looking as you would never look twice at an ugly duckling like me. It was silly for me to hope you might like me for who I am, not what I look like."

He was stunned. She cared for him? "I should not have said what I did to my brother. I was an arse." He pulled her onto his lap. "It was fear. The king's men will come, I worry what will happen to you." He stroked her hair. "You rescued me from the tower. The moment I saw you, I thought you were a fairy come to take me away. Anna. I do want you here. I would give all I possess to have someone such as you."

He kissed her hair, mumbling words of love.

"You are kind and thoughtful. Your skin like fine ivory. The many colors in your hair remind me of the countryside. How can you not see how beautiful you are?"

She sniffed. "You don't mean it. You're only saying it because you feel like a big jerk."

Jerk. Charlotte called his brother such a word. He knew 'twas not flattering.

"I have been too wrapped up in my own cares. I do know what it's like to be separated from those you love."

He held up a hand. "I know mine was by choice and yours is not. I do have some understanding of what you feel."

"You're only saying these things because you want me to come back without making a fuss. But don't you see? After what Charlotte told me, I have to believe there is a small chance I can go back. And I must try. If I can't get back then at least I will know I have done everything in my power to try. But if I don't try..."

She looked up at him her green eyes full of tears. "I cannot live with myself if I don't try."

"You have my word. Once we get back, I'll send word to my brothers letting them know where we are going, I will take you back to the tower."

She started to protest, and John said, "I do not delay on purpose. But we must have a fresh horse and pack provisions. My brothers needs know so if anything happens to me, they will know to come for you."

"Oh. That's very kind. I won't forget all you've done for me."

Seeing the pain in her eyes, her need to go home, John made a choice. He would not tell her he was in love with her. He would think of her instead of himself. And he would let her go. Though he would remember her all of his days.

As they rode through the gates of Blackmoor, John saw a commotion in the courtyard.

"'Tis time you are back."

He dismounted and lifted Anna off the horse. John turned to his eldest brother.

"'Tis good to see you, Edward." Was all he got out before Edward's fist met his face.

John struck back. As he and his brother exchanged blows, he heard Robert's voice.

"'Tis too early to brawl." Robert yawned.

Men watched, calling out helpful suggestions and insults.

"This is silly."

"Aye, lady. Men will be boys no matter how old they are."

She rolled her eyes. "Whatever."

Edward spat blood onto the ground. "Seems I am arrived just in time. The roof looks likely to fall on your heads."

"I am sorry I did not tell you I was alive."

Edward clapped him on the shoulder. "I know you thought you were keeping all of us safe. I have missed you, John."

"And I you." John cleared his throat, willing the feelings to go away.

"What news do you bring?"

Edward looked askance at Anna, who was sitting on the other side of him.

"Say what you will. I have told her the tale."

Edward raised his brows. "All you know about him and still you enjoy his company, lady?"

Anna leaned forward across John and looked at Edward, a saucy grin on her face.

"All of you Thorntons are so handsome I find I quite lose my head whenever I'm around you."

Edward grinned. "Careful, this one here may actually lose his."

Anna looked horrified for a moment until she realized they were teasing. If you couldn't make fun of something, what was the point of living?

"So what are you going to do to help him?"

"I quite like her."

"I'm growing old, Edward."

Edward rolled his eyes. "'Tis not welcome news. The king is only seventeen. Denby has his ear and his wife is young. Denby parades her in front of the king hoping he will make her his mistress."

"What about Letitia?"

"Have you not heard? Letitia died three years ago from fever. Denby married again a month later."

"Then why does he come for me? Why does he care?"

Edward shook his head. "He cared not for his wife. They couldn't stand each other. But he is a prideful man and seeks to strike back at you."

His brother was much as John remembered. Full of energy and unable to sit still. When he was thinking, he had to pace. All the Thorntons did.

"What do we do?"

"Denby is on a diplomatic mission. While he is gone, I will seek an audience with the king. Try to reason with him." Edward scratched at his chin. "And offer him gold."

Chapter Twenty-Six

Anna had now met all of John's brothers except Christian. If things could be different...if she didn't have to get back to her father, she could be happy here. She was surprised at how quickly she'd adapted to living without modern-day conveniences.

While she still thought longingly of hot showers, flipping the switch for power, ice cream, pizza, movies, and modern-day transportation, she had grown used to life here. And really, what was the use of complaining? It wasn't like she could change anything.

Each one of his brothers was as breathtakingly handsome as the other. And they all were charming and kind. She wondered what Charlotte was doing. It felt good to have made a friend. Not just a friend, a sister. Charlotte assured her Lucy and Melinda were just as delightful. That they would welcome her with open arms. To have three friends would be more than she had in her life in Florida. Working all the time, she said no to most invitations. After a while, people stopped asking. It had taken Anna a long time to notice the invitations stopped. By the time she did, it was too late to do anything about it. Only Hattie remained.

She couldn't even have a pet. Working so much wouldn't be fair to an animal. When she was little, she had a dog and a cat. It would have been comforting to come home to a furry baby. Sometimes she talked to herself when there was no one else around. At least if she talked to a dog or cat, people wouldn't think she was crazy.

She snorted.

"Is something amiss, mistress?"

"What?" Anna stretched. "No. I was just thinking." She looked at the fabric in her hands. Her flower looked more like an abstract squiggle. The young girl teaching her to embroider...hers looked like something in a museum.

The girl frowned. "Mayhap if we try..."

"No. It's hopeless, but thank you for trying to show me. Run along. I'm going to pull weeds."

In a perfect world, her dad would be healthy and she would bring him to the past with her. He'd like it here. The fresh air and people. Too bad life rarely worked out the way you thought it should.

Like John. She wanted to believe he found her attractive, like he'd said he did, that he saw her for the person she was inside, but it was hard. She wasn't being hard on herself; she'd seen how men coming into the diner hit on the other waitresses. No one ever hit on her. And if they did, it seemed like a token gesture. To think someone like him could find someone like her interesting and pretty turned her world upside down. She firmly believed actions spoke louder than words. So she would watch him and decide.

In the morning, Anna woke to the sound of men's voices. The mason and his men were hard at work. She felt useless. She could sew, but only with a machine. And yesterday she'd found out she was dreadful at hand stitching. Anna didn't even cook. She ate at the diner on the weekends, and during the week usually grabbed a frozen meal and threw it in the microwave. Pressed for time, she never found the time to cook a meal from scratch.

Everything in her life seemed to move faster and faster, and she always felt like she was falling behind. The couple of times she'd tried to help in the kitchen, she caused more trouble than she'd helped.

There was one thing she was good at—pulling weeds. Once she had someone show her what was a weed and what wasn't, she passed her time pulling weeds to get the various small gardens ready to be planted. There would be flower, vegetable, herb, and medicinal gardens. There were tons of weeds to pull. Seeing them pile up made her feel a useful member of Blackmoor.

Anna sat back on her heels and looked up at the sun.

"I thought I might find you here." John knelt down and handed her a cup.

"Water for you, wine for me."

She drank deeply. "You remembered."

He stretched out on the ground beside her.

"How is your arm?"

She blushed. "You heard what happened in the kitchen."

He turned his head, but she could see the smile tugging at the corners of his lips.

"I think everyone heard."

"I thought I was dumping the soup into the cauldron. How was I to know the handle would fall off?" She saw his shoulders shaking. "I know you're trying not to laugh. But go ahead. It is kind of funny."

He held his side, laughing. "They told me when the soup hit the floor, it covered everyone around you. But not a drop on you. I can see them with chunks of vegetables in their hair, dripping on the floor." He laughed again, and she laughed with him.

"I think I should stay out of the kitchen. That's why I'm out here. One of the girls showed me what was a weed and what wasn't, so I'm pulling weeds." She gave him a rueful smile. "I figure I can't do too much harm out here."

"Did no one teach you how to cook? To run a household?"

Anna shook her head. "No. My parents always struggled to make ends meet. There was never really enough money to go around, but somehow they scrimped and saved enough money for me to go to community college. We ate a lot of easy meals. Things like pasta and casseroles and frozen dinners. I never learned to cook. It's not something you have to learn. And like I was telling you before, I went to a shop to buy clothing already made, so I never learned to sew."

She yanked a clump of weeds and added it to the growing pile beside her. "I think I'm rather useless as far as skills go around here."

"You are a lady. You do not need to know how to sew or to cook. As to managing a household, 'tis a skill that can be learned. Do not ever say you are not useful. I can think of no one else who could have rescued me from the tower. You must stop saying such things about yourself. 'Tis time you accept your own worth."

"Women in my time are expected to be beautiful with amazing bodies. There's so much pressure to be and look a certain way." She touched his hand. "I'm trying to change."

Anna leaned back and looked at him. "I heard some of the men talking. Are you sure there wasn't anyone left from your camp in the woods?"

John let out a long sigh and was quiet for so long that Anna felt bad for asking. But she knew how he felt: the weight of responsibility weighing so heavily on your shoulders that sometimes you thought it would crush you to the ground.

"Nay. Rabbie survived. He works in the stables at Highworth. Robert will be good to him. My healer stayed and perished with those who were ill. I have sent many inquiries, but the soldiers did their work well. None survived. If by chance any did survive, they are likely still in hiding and may never find me. At least not until they know if I will live or die."

She reached up and touched his cheek, feeling the stubble. How many times had someone seen that look on her face? Before she could think better of it, Anna leaned down and lightly brushed her lips over John's. His lips were firm and he smelled like horses and green things. She leaned back, keeping her eyes closed, afraid she would open them and see a look of disgust on his face.

"Open your eyes, Anna," John said softly.

She opened one eye and then the other, not daring to say a word.

"I would gladly find myself imprisoned again for one of your kisses, freely given."

And didn't that just make her go weak in the knees?

Chapter Twenty-Seven

All through supper that night, Anna kept touching her face. She couldn't believe she'd found the confidence to kiss John. It was the first time in her life she'd ever kissed a man first. And he hadn't pulled away or had a disgusted look on his face. He said he'd go to prison to kiss her again. Was it possible? Was she really not as unattractive as she thought? Her worldview shifted ever so slightly.

She had trouble sleeping. Tossing and turning, thinking about him. The two of them together. What her life might be like if she stayed. In the end, she decided it would be up to the fates to decide. She would try to go back, and if she could she would. She owed it to her dad. But if she couldn't, then she would know she had done all she could, and she would make a life here with a clear conscience.

After being stuck in the bog, she was hesitant to wear a dress to travel. John argued with her, but after she told him her fears, he gave in. She braided her hair down her back, and wore the tunic and hose she had swiped before. How the women got them clean was magic in her book. John assured her the boy had been given a new set of clothes. And when she fessed up about the gold, he smiled. Said he expected her to do nothing less. How would she purchase food and lodging along the way if she didn't have money?

Full from breakfast, she waited in the courtyard for John to appear. The horses were ready—she would ride her horse this time. The thought made her a little bit nervous, but she was willing to try. It was time to try new things.

She offered a carrot to Black Horse. "I'm going to trust you know what you're doing. So you're in control, but don't throw me off and we'll be fine, okay?"

The horse twitched an ear, contentedly munching the carrot.

As John approached, she saw he wore his cloak, which was odd, given how warm it was today.

"I know we're leaving today...if you come back, he will be waiting for you."

From under the cloak, he produced a small brown dog. The dog ran around in circles when he set it on the ground. He was adorable with his tail wagging a hundred miles a minute and his floppy tan ears. He licked her hand.

"I've never had a dog before. He's very small. Is he a baby?"

"'Tis not quite a year old. I thought he would be company for you."

When she stood up, wiping her face where the dog had licked her, she saw him watching her.

He spoke in a low voice so no one else would hear. "I know you want to go home, so I wish it for you too. The man could not afford to feed the dog, so I took him. Trust I will take good care of him when you are gone."

Anna patted the dog, stroking the soft fur. "You're a beautiful boy. Be good." She leaned down, kissing him on the top of his head.

"Thank you. It was very kind of you."

As they made their way through the moors, Anna tensed. It wasn't until they were away and had traveled another hour or so that she felt like she could relax. The horse was content to follow along or walk beside John's horse.

"While the countryside is beautiful, I'm already sick

and tired of this journey."

"Do not worry. I will not let you fall into another bog."

"At least this time I'm with someone who knows how to make a fire. And we have horses."

"And do not forget. You have me to protect you."

She smiled at him. "How could I forget?"

They stopped for a late lunch. Afterward, Anna looked for a place to relieve herself. She heard the sound of running water and followed it, happy to find a place to refill her water jug.

During the afternoon, she'd been surprised at how few people they encountered. If it was a well-traveled road, then they saw a good number of people. But on smaller paths, they might not see anyone. Most were friendly, though some seemed wary. And she could understand why John wanted to avoid everyone. More soldiers had been spotted nearby. They were closing in. Yesterday, she'd seen his face on a broadsheet in a town they had to pass through. When she pointed it out, he brushed her concerns away.

"None this close to Blackmoor will turn us in. They are loyal, or at least I hope they are."

That night as they made camp, she watched how he started the fire.

"I don't think I'll ever be able to do that."

"I will start your fires, my lady."

They talked deep into the night until Anna found

herself yawning and barely able to keep her eyes open.

"Go to sleep. I will take first watch."

She didn't think she answered him before she was asleep.

Chapter Twenty-Eight

Wasn't it the same with everything? Anna had been afraid to ride by herself. But the more distance they covered, the more she enjoyed riding. She had an entirely new appreciation for horses. Sure, cars were so much faster, but people might not be as stressed out in her own time if they rode a horse to work. A quiet giggle escaped.

Instead of bring your child to work day or bring your pet to work day, it could be ride your horse to work day. With stables and pastures next to office buildings instead of bike racks.

Daydreaming about popsicles and milkshakes, she jerked in the saddle as the horse came to a sudden stop

"Why are we stopping?"

John put a finger to his lips. "Silence."

He dismounted, helped her off the horse, and leaned forward. For a moment she thought he was going to kiss her again.

Then he whispered in her ear, "Soldiers. Close. Follow me."

The kiss would have been better. No matter how she strained, Anna didn't hear anything. John had lived as an outlaw for a long time and obviously knew what he was doing. She followed as he led the horses into the woods. He found an area with fallen brush and a patch of grass, making a natural screen. He tied the horses to the trees.

"We will move the branches. They will conceal the horses."

Anna had to admit, it looked pretty convincing. "Won't the horses make noise?"

"Not enough to be heard. We will conceal ourselves over there."

How was it possible the man could move without making a sound? She, on the other hand, sounded like a herd of elephants, as she trailed him through the brush. No matter how gingerly she stepped, a twig cracked, sounding like a gunshot, or she made some other horribly loud noise. But no one came galloping after them, so maybe she wasn't as loud as she sounded to her own ears.

John led her around an outcropping of stone and pointed to the base, where she could make out a small, shallow opening.

"You want to hide there? What about snakes?"

"There are no snakes. We will be safe." He pulled her down onto the ground. "Do you trust me to keep you from harm?"

"Of course I do. Snakes are a completely different story. If you had seen the size of some of the snakes we have in Florida, you'd be taking me more seriously."

He put a finger to his lips and whispered, "You can tell me all about the wee beasties once we are safe."

Anna shut her mouth, but not before sticking her tongue out at him. His mouth twitched. It looked like he was biting his cheek to hold back the laughter. Annoying man.

They pulled brush in front of the opening and waited. Anna hoped she wouldn't need to go to the bathroom. As soon as she had the thought, of course she had to go. Knowing it was purely psychological didn't make the urge go away. Wearing a dress would have made things easier. None of the women wore undergarments. You spread your legs and went. Could go wherever you wanted. But now she was basically wearing leggings, there was no way she could pull them down to go. Then again, she wouldn't have peed in a dress scrunched into a small hole with John either.

You'll just have to wait. You will never live it down if you pee your pants in front of the man you're crazy about.

A touch on her arm made her twitch. His lips brushed her ear. "They are close."

The crack of a twig made her mouth go dry. She heard the sounds of horses and the low voices of men. There were several voices, but she couldn't make out how many. The horses made it sound like a large group.

Anna strained to see through the brush. Just when she thought her eyes were playing tricks on her, she spotted the men. All dressed similarly, and many wore serious expressions. Her heart beat faster, pounding in her chest. *Please don't let them hear.* For it certainly seemed as loud as a drum at a rock concert to her ears. Her throat dry, she swallowed several times so she wouldn't cough.

The space was narrow, and John was pressed against her so tightly she felt the tension in the stiffness of his body, which made her even more nervous. What would happen if the horses made a noise?

She was dying to ask but didn't dare. The soldiers were so close. She could smell the horses. The sweat of men who hadn't washed in a long while. Her stomach heaving, Anna pressed her lips together so as not to make a sound. *You will not barf.*

If she reached out, she could touch the leg of the man closest to her. Her breathing slowed, and she tried to remember a meditation class she'd taken a long time ago. Every molecule was focused on keeping quiet.

She'd seen the cells in the tower up close and

personal, and while she wanted to get back so she could go home, Anna had no desire to be a guest. The soldiers' voices sounded loud even though she knew they were speaking in normal tones. Everything sounded louder when it was quiet. Did they know how close they were to their quarry?

"Water the horses and rest for a bit. The Thornton bastard can't be far."

No. They couldn't be stopping right here. But as she watched, the men dismounted, some of them pulling food out of packs, others leading the horses off for a drink. A few sat down, stretching out their legs. One of the men leaned against a rock next to them, so close she could make out the color of his eyes.

If the man shifted his body less than a foot, he would lean right into them. Anna could see the hand stitching on his clothing. The gray in the beard on his face. If the man turned his head, he could see them hidden behind the brush.

It was as if she was hyperaware of their surroundings. Every sound magnified, every color brighter. Pain radiated down her arm. For a moment she panicked, thinking she was having a heart attack. Rationally, she knew she wasn't, but she couldn't figure out what was wrong until she realized she was pressing so tightly against the rock that her arm had fallen asleep. As the tension left her body, a sigh escaped. Anna pressed a hand over her mouth. The man leaning against the rock shifted as if he felt the air, but didn't turn. Talk about a close call.

How did John do it? He was as motionless and still as the stone surrounding them. Men came and went, leading the horses to drink, eating and making jokes. A small part of her wanted to talk with them. Everyone she'd met so far fascinated her. After all, how often did you get to travel to another time? And talk with the people. Hear about their daily lives, hopes, fears, and dreams.

The soldiers were men doing a job. She was pretty sure it wasn't personal, but all the same, she had no interest in going to prison.

A soldier approached the man leaning against the rock, who had fallen asleep. He nudged the man with his boot.

"'Tis time. Get up, Ned."

The man grunted and got to his feet. "Hold on. Need to take a piss."

As the soldier moved away, the one called Ned turned, reached in his pants, pulled it out, and started peeing. Anna almost called out; in fact, she would have if John hadn't clapped a hand over her mouth, seeming to know what was about to happen.

She looked at him and he looked at her. Saw the humor in his eyes. Pee spattered through the brush and landed on their feet. His body shook but he made no sound.

It wasn't funny at all. It was completely disgusting. She'd never been peed on in her entire life. And, quite frankly, Anna didn't think she'd ever get the sight of the man's junk out of her mind. It was something that couldn't be unseen. Not to mention he smelled and his little snake looked like he didn't wash very often.

He finished, set himself to rights, and turned round, making his way back to the group of men. It seemed to take hours before all the men were mounted and riding out of the wood. Even when she could no longer hear them, John kept a hand on her arm, holding her still. He shook his head, so he must have heard them, even though she couldn't hear a thing.

Finally he released her. He moved the brush away, staying quiet. Somehow she managed not to run screaming for the water. Instead she waited, trusting he would let her know when it was all clear.

She followed John, stepping where he stepped, as they made their way across the open space to where the horses were hidden. She couldn't believe none of the soldiers had spotted the animals. Guess they were far enough away.

When John moved the brush aside, Anna saw them contentedly munching on a patch of grass. She looked at him, raising her eyebrows, and he nodded.

"Oh my gosh, I have never been peed on. Never, in my entire life. I don't think I will ever forget it." She choked out before bursting into laughter, so hard that tears ran down her face and her stomach hurt. John laughed, his eyes twinkling, the deep sound echoing across the wood.

"My apologies the lady had to see such a sight...even though 'twas rather small."

They were still laughing as they made their way to the water. Anna scrubbed at her boots and hose to remove the spots. Once done, she drank her fill. Helping her on the horse, he touched her knee, the heat traveling to her stomach.

"We shall ride for a few hours before we stop for the night, to put distance between us and them."

"I think I've been scarred for life. I'll never be able to go the bathroom outside again without being worried someone is nearby, watching."

He looked at her, the corners of his mouth twitching. "Makes one beware the woods, aye?"

Chapter Twenty-Nine

The more time John spent with Anna, the more he yearned to keep her by his side forever. After the close call with the soldiers, they rode hard the rest of the day, stopping only when it was too dark.

She helped him make camp. He couldn't resist. "Tell me about the snakes."

Her face burned.

"You mean the solider?" She gave him an odd look, and he realized she had called the man's member a snake.

He responded with a rude jest, though in Norman French so she wouldn't think him uncouth. John grinned.

"The lady has a wicked mind. Not *that* snake. The beasties you said live in Florida."

Pink spread across her neck and face, making her eyes sparkle.

"Oh, I knew that."

He resisted the urge to tease, instead waiting for her to tell him about the creatures.

"In Florida, there's a large swampy area." She shuddered. "Not unlike a bog with shallow water hiding all kinds of things. There are more than a million alligators in Florida alone. Many other warm states now have alligators in bodies of fresh water."

"So many. And they can eat a man? Are they hunted and eaten?"

She wrinkled up her nose, which he noticed she did whenever she was thinking. How this woman could think she wasn't beautiful was beyond his reasoning. She had the clearest green eyes, reminding him of a summer meadow, and her skin was so soft and smooth that he constantly found himself aching to touch her.

"They're usually shy creatures. But yes, some have eaten humans. And if someone's pet gets too close to the water, an alligator will snatch it. I rather like them. I always have, ever since I was a child. So I wish they weren't hunted, though I understand why they are. Yes, people do eat them. I never have. To me it would be like eating your pet, though people say they taste like chicken. And shoes, belts, wallets, and purses are made from their hides."

She turned a deeper shade of pink, making him

wonder what she was going to say.

"I told you I used to sing to them when I was little. And I fed them marshmallows."

"What did you sing?"

He could imagine Anna as a small child, her shimmering hair blowing in the breeze as she sang to the beast. The animals would be so enchanted by her voice that they would not eat her.

"And what are marshmallows?"

"My voice isn't very good, but I love to sing when I'm alone. It's one of the things I miss about being here. I used to get in my car, turn up the radio, and sing. When I was little, I didn't have a favorite song; I would sing whatever song I liked at the moment. Though I mostly made up really silly songs to sing to the alligators. We had a dock that went out over the water and I used to sit on the edge, my legs crossed, and stare into the water, singing as if I could conjure them up from the depths. And it always seemed within a few minutes, one of the alligators would surface. He would sort of rock back and forth in the water, listening to me. He would come almost to the dock and what I know now about them..."

She shuddered, as if remembering something unpleasant.

"What do you know now?"

"Alligators can jump their length. And many of the alligators in the water behind our house were between six and fourteen feet long. So any of them could have easily jumped up and snatched me off the dock to eat me."

"But none of the beasts ever did. They were so enchanted by your voice. Knew you loved them so they would not eat you. Even if you fell in, they would not eat you. One of the great creatures would let you climb on his back and take you to safety."

She laughed. "And I thought I was the one with the fanciful imagination. I used to think that's what would happen. You don't know how desperately I wished I could swim with them. That they would let me ride on their back. I... Oh my." Anna covered her mouth, trying to hold in her laughter.

"What?"

"Promise you won't tell him?"

"Aye. Who?"

"Henry."

John was perplexed. What did Henry have to do with alligators?

"I had a favorite alligator. He was twelve feet long and only had one eye. When I sang to him sometimes he would roll, showing me his belly, and he'd come up to the edge of the dock. But the funny part is...I named him Henry."

John grinned. "Your secret is safe with me."

She handed him a peach and sat close to the fire he'd built up.

Before he took a bite, he looked at the fruit. He'd

seen her arse when she undressed. It reminded him of a peach. John shifted from foot to foot.

"What are marshmallows?"

"They're hard to explain." She looked around, picked up a rock, and held it in her palm. "The big ones are about this big, and white in color. The little ones, more like the size of a pebble."

Anna tossed the rock aside. "When you bite into a marshmallow, well, it's sort of like biting into a cloud. Airy and sweet. It's really hard to explain. I'd try to make them for you, but I don't think I could re-create them, especially since I'm a terrible cook."

She snorted. "They don't have much of a taste, but for some reason the alligators loved them. Marshmallows float. So I would throw one into the water, and when the alligator surfaced he would slowly swim over...then *snap*, the marshmallow was gone in a second. It was the most amazing sight to a child, and I would laugh and clap my hands every time they ate one."

When she was talking about something that made her happy, she lit up from within. He knew there was no woman in the whole of England more beautiful than she.

"If we ran out of the big marshmallows, I'd have to take the small ones."

Her face turned sad. "My mother used to get so mad at me for taking all the marshmallows. She played cards and always took a dessert with marshmallows. And I was always taking them. We bought bagfuls."

He was trying to imagine what the food tasted like. "Are marshmallows served for dinner?"

"You don't eat them as a meal. They are more of a garnish. Like adding carrots to stew. The carrot isn't the whole meal...bad example. For some people carrots are a meal. The marshmallow is a topping. And the little ones, the alligators would eat them, but I don't think they liked them as much because it was more work for them to chomp all the little pieces."

John wanted to ask her more about alligators and the large snakes she said were in Florida. Before he could ask, he sensed movement.

John threw Anna to the ground, covering her with his body. Pressed against her, he felt the length of her against him. For a moment he wanted to stay like this forever. He said quietly, "We are not alone. Stay still."

He drew the dagger from his boot and rolled to his feet, the other hand on the sword at his hip, crouched in front of her, to protect her with his body. They had stone at their back. The enemy would have to meet him first.

"Show yourself, whoreson."

The old woman stepping out into the firelight could not have surprised him more.

"You live. Rabbie said all perished in the fire."

Magda's eyes gleamed. When she grinned, he could see she was now missing a tooth on the side of her mouth. She cackled as she said, "'Tis not so easy as all that to kill me."

She turned to gaze upon Anna. "Who have we here?"

Chapter Thirty

Magda eased herself down by the fire as Anna watched the old woman's every move. John's healer and friend looked like she stepped out of a fairy tale. She was a healer—some would say witch, others demon. The woman was skilled in herbs and he had no fear of her.

"It will take more than those men to kill me." She wiped her eyes. "We lost so many. All those too sick to travel. I could not save them. I should have listened to you and moved them sooner."

He laid a hand on her arm, the skin soft as velvet and wrinkled with age.

"You were right not to move them, you cannot have known we would be betrayed. 'Twas Archie."

"He will get what he deserves in the next life. 'Tis said you took him down with one strike of your blade."

"Denby's blade. I thought it fitting. I will kill Denby and every man who was there. I will track down and find them all."

"After you are safe." She patted his knee. "Forty are safe and in hiding." Magda paused, making John wonder what was coming next.

"The ones who survived. They all know who you are. That you are one of the Thornton brothers."

"Do they despise me?"

"Why would you say such a thing?"

"Why? A noble who pretends to be like them, who kills, ransoms, and steals from other nobles? They must think me a hypocrite."

"They love you more. That you would give up your birthright to live among them. They consider you one of them."

John ran his hands through his hair. The feelings within made it hard to speak. He pretended to wipe dust from his hose to give himself a moment to trust his voice would not waver.

"Wearing the mask let me be another person. The bandit of the wood. Now...I am simply John Thornton. A man with no title. My presence puts those around me in grave danger. I no longer have anything to offer."

Anna and Magda protested at the same time.

John held up a hand. "Let me wallow for a while."

"There is no need," Anna said. "You are a good person. I can think of so many people who would not have done anything to help those less fortunate. People who walk by and pretend not to see what is right in front of them. I am proud of you." Anna leaned over and kissed him on the cheek.

He pulled her into his lap, twining her hair through his fingers. He never tired of looking at the colors, feeling the silkiness against his skin. John needed to see his people with his own eyes to know they were unharmed. Needed to hear each one say they wanted him by their side. If they would accept, he would bring each one to Blackmoor to rebuild their lives.

"Where are they?"

Magda looked to Anna, who met her gaze without flinching.

"I trust her with my life."

The old woman nodded. "We are in hiding near the border."

"Nay, Magda. 'Tis too close to the fighting. Send them to Edward. He will take them in."

She scowled. "You cannot. You have been gone, not wishing to hear of your brothers. I respected your wishes. But you do not understand. Your brother will take Denby's place as advisor to the king. He cannot harbor outlaws even if one of them is his brother."

"How do you know this?"

"You ask me this after all our years together?" She turned her palms up, looking at the lines. "I know. Heed my words, John Thornton. Your brother will become even more important than he is now."

He blew out a breath. "Then send them to Blackmoor. Unless you have foreseen my death and the destruction of my home?"

She squinted at him, a crafty look in her eye as she took his and Anna's hand in hers.

"You will be a great leader to your people. They will make a life at Blackmoor." Magda turned her gaze to Anna. "You have lost much, child. You are young. The child should not be the parent."

The old woman stared into the fire. John saw the questions on Anna's face as she watched every move Magda made.

The healer came back to herself. "The choices you both make will determine your destiny." She pressed her palm to his cheek. "Blackmoor will stand with you as its lord."

"Will you come? Live at Blackmoor and be its healer?"

"Aye. I'm getting too old to sleep in the woods."

They continued to talk, Anna sitting there quietly, listening. When John looked over later, she had fallen asleep. Magda caught his look.

"She is not of our world."

"Nay. She is from the future. I believe her. The tales she has told me."

"There is someone waiting who she cares for a great deal. A man she yearns to go home to. The only reason she wishes to leave you."

"Her father. He is very ill, and without her wages, he will be homeless." John wasn't sure he wanted to know: "Can she go back?"

"Who knows what the fates decide? You love her." Sharp, piercing eyes looked into his heart. "She is the first woman you have ever truly loved."

John gave her a sharp look.

"She sleeps. Do not worry; she does not hear us."

"I do love her. More than my own life. But I cannot tell her. She must make her own decision to go back or to stay. If she could go back and did not because of me, she would grow to hate me later."

Magda patted his face as if he were a small child.

"You are a good man. And you are well matched for each other."

Magda rolled up in her cloak and went to sleep. John didn't know how long he stayed up staring into the fire. When he woke in the morning, she was gone.

Anna rolled over, stretching. When she sat up and looked around, she said, "Where is she?"

"She'll go to the others. And a few at a time will make their way to Blackmoor."

"Will they be in danger?"

"They are used to being unseen."

"I can relate."

Chapter Thirty-One

If Anna never had to get on another horse, she'd be happy. The first few days had been fine, but now she was tired of riding. Tired of traveling. All she wanted was a bed, a hot bath, and a semi-warm meal.

Didn't it just figure she had to go to the bathroom? Again. After squirming for a while, she finally broke down.

"Can we stop for a couple minutes?"

He seemed distracted. "I thought we would eat while we rode. We should continue on."

Well, that was all nice and good for him, but she had to go now. She tried thinking of deserts and airplane bathrooms, which were the worst. Anna would rather hold it than use the restroom on a plane. She always worried something would happen and she'd get sucked down the hole and ejected into thin air. It was no use.

"I'm really sorry, but I need to stop. You know, womanly things." Heat blossomed across her chest and sweat trickled down her side. Everyone went to the bathroom. Why was she embarrassed? And yet something about telling the man you were falling for that you needed to go pee just took any possible romance out of the situation.

"My apologies. I should have looked to your needs earlier."

He led the horses off the path. As he lifted her down, she was aware of everything about him. Up close, she could see flecks of gold in the brown of his eyes. He had amazing, thick lashes. Talk about envious. Why did men get the lush eyelashes when women had to spend a fortune over their lifetime on mascara?

He held her in front of him, her feet dangling several inches off the ground. Everything around them went still. Just when she thought he'd kiss her again, instead he dropped her to the ground.

John's hand went to the hilt at his side. "Listen."

What now? She knew the drill. Be quiet. Don't make a sound. He closed his eyes, listening. After several minutes he opened his eyes. Tucking a lock of hair behind her ear, he traced her lips with his thumb.

"'Tis nothing. But make haste; I do not wish to linger."

Anna looked around for a place to conceal herself.

Off to her right she saw a clump of trees and brush.

"I'm going over there."

"Quickly, Anna."

The man was half camel. She swore he could ride all day without stopping. How did he manage? Did it come with living life on the run? From being a warrior? Or was it just that he had the bladder of a camel?

She found a spot, lifted her dress, and squatted. She had washed out the tunic and hose and changed into the dress. As they got closer to London they'd see more people, and she didn't want to stick out as a woman in men's clothing.

Toilet paper. Boy, that was another thing she missed. Anna wiggled and shook a bit. Turning to her left, she caught a flash of green behind a tree.

Anna didn't even have a chance to scream before she found herself surrounded by four men. The fifth one hauled her roughly against him, his hand covering her mouth and part of her nose. She couldn't breathe. Anna struggled and kicked. The man squeezed her wrist so hard, she heard the bones crack.

"Shut yer mouth, before I gut ye like a pig."

Instead of obeying, she stomped on his foot. He cursed but didn't let her go. There was a sharp prick at the base of her ear.

"You may not be much to look at, but when I'm finished with you, no one will look at you."

There was an odd smell in the air. Something

coppery. It took her a moment to sink in. It was blood. Her blood, trickling down her neck.

Just like an afternoon thunderstorm in Florida, the skies opened up. The wind blowing and all hell broke loose. Anna watched the first man fall to the ground. What was happening? A flash caught her eye. John's blade flashed again. He was moving so fast she could hardly see the sword. Another man screamed and went down, clutching his midsection. She saw red and had to turn away.

The rational part of her brain knew the skirmish hadn't lasted that long, but she'd swear it had gone on forever. The sheets of rain made it hard to see. She thought there were four men on the ground. The man holding her was shaking, the knife at her throat wiggling, making her so nervous she was afraid to swallow. Afraid it would slip and she would die.

John was soaking wet, looking like some mythical warrior appearing out of the mist. The look on his face was so frightening, if she had seen the same look when she was in the tower, she would have never set him free. Seeing him like this? She could see why he had deserved his outlaw title and why so many feared him.

His voice cut across the storm, so calm she knew there must be an incredible amount of rage behind it. He did not meet her gaze, as if he could not spare an ounce of kindness while in full battle mode.

"Anna. I need you to listen to my voice."

The knife tightened against her throat. "Don't talk to her. Shut your mouth. We was paid well to take you. Dead or alive, my lord does not care."

"And who might your lord be?"

"Lord Denby. He sent us after you and the wench."

"He'll have to wait a little longer." He flicked his gaze to her. "Duck."

She bit down on the hand covering her mouth. The man yelped and yanked his hand away, and Anna let all her weight fall. There was an odd-sounding thunk. When she turned around, Anna saw the knife sticking out of the man's eye. That, combined with the four men on the ground, was more than her stomach could take. She leaned over, one hand holding her hair, the other braced on her knees as she heaved the contents of her stomach into the grass.

"Anna, run."

A man dropped out of the tree. As John struck him down, she ran for the horses. She'd only gone a short distance when someone else grabbed her. Okra fudge! How many were there? Were they multiplying like rabbits?

The blow struck her in the face, snapping her head back. A loud ringing filled her ears. Anna tasted blood. Her lip burned. She touched a finger to it. He had split her lip. She had never raised her hand against anyone. Squinting, she aimed for the side of his face, raking her nails down as hard as she could. The man howled and slugged her in the eye. She fell back, crying out in pain.

The man sat on top of her, making it difficult to breathe.

"I'll at least have some fun with you before I kill you."

Anna sucked in as much breath as she could and screamed for all she was worth. "John!"

He was there in an instant, his sword flashing down to take the man's head off, when a voice rang out.

"Put down the sword or she dies."

How he managed, Anna didn't know, but the blade came to a stop a hair away from the man's neck and stayed there, vibrating.

A man strode forward. He motioned to his left. She counted three archers with arrows pointed at her. Another group of men rode into the clearing.

John kept the sword at the man's neck. He stood there, anger visible on his face and throughout the lines in his body.

"Remove the blade."

John cursed but did so. The man in charge snarled at the man sitting on top of her.

"Get off."

The man rolled off her. She yanked her dress down and sat up. He limped away, which made her happy. And now he had three long, nasty scratches down the side of his face. Her eye and lip felt hot to the touch. A black eye. She'd never had one. And a fat lip to match.

"Get her up."

Two men dragged her to her feet. Others shoved John to his knees. There were too many for him to fight back. One of the men grabbed his hair and yanked his head up.

"Watch."

A sick feeling ran through Anna. They held her as the leader strode forward.

"I told you to remove your blade and you did not, swine." The man had brown hair and a scar that made him look like he was sneering. He leaned in, his bad breath almost sending her to her knees.

"Move and you die."

He raised a dagger, bringing it down at the back of her head. Her head jerked. When she felt the air on the back of her neck, she knew. He had cut her hair off.

The strands floated away on the wind. Out of the corner of her eye, she saw John punch the man closest to him, swearing. She didn't know what he said, but whenever he spoke in multiple languages, she knew he was cursing.

"Take her," the leader barked as he strode over and bonked John on the head with the hilt of his blade. He crumpled to the ground. The soldiers kicked and punched him. She saw him reaching out, trying to grab hold of something, but she couldn't tell what. It was too hard to see from the tears streaming down her face.

Chapter Thirty-Two

Why must it always rain when he was locked in a cage? But this time John's head rested not on hard wood but on something soft. He opened his eyes to see Anna looking down at him, concern on her face. His head rested in her lap as she ran her fingers through his hair.

The wind blew and he could see the pale skin of her neck.

"Can you ever forgive me?" he croaked out.

"For what?"

"I cannot keep you safe." He reached up, touching the ragged ends. "Your beautiful hair. So many shades of color. Like sunlight and earth."

She reached a hand up, touching what remained. He saw the sorrow on her face.

"I've always had long hair. Ever since I was a child."

She touched a finger to the strands, trying and failing to tuck it behind her ear. "I feel lighter somehow, though I bet my neck will be cold this winter."

"'Tis my fault."

"Why? You did nothing wrong. You saved me from those men. I hate to think what would've happened if I had been alone. It's me who should be asking you for forgiveness. If we'd stayed at Blackmoor, none of this would have happened."

"Nay. They would have come for us there."

He touched her hair again. She looked even younger with it shorn off.

"Don't worry. It's only hair. It'll grow back."

He wanted to talk with her, but his head pained him terribly, and against his will, his eyes drifted shut.

John woke, shivering and sneezing. Anna touched his forehead and then her own. He felt awfully warm to her.

"I am well."

"You're grumpy."

He made a sound in the back of his throat.

"You know men make the worst patients. They're

always whining and complaining like they're dying."

He cracked one eye open, scowling at her. "If you will not tend me, tell me about the snakes in Florida. To take my mind off my aching head."

She rubbed his shoulders as she talked. The motion of the wagon and the rain falling on them lulled her into a state between wakefulness and dreams.

"In Florida there are several kinds of snakes. The poisonous ones are the cottonmouth and rattlesnakes. If they bite, you can die, but there's an antidote. Then there are pythons and boa constrictors." Even talking about them made Anna feel creepy crawly all over. "I hate them all. In my book the only good snake is a dead snake."

"I have seen a snake. Most folks say they are the devil's familiar."

She totally agreed. "I can believe it. Pythons are not native to Florida. Someone brought them there and now they're causing problems in the Everglades. Remember, the Everglades are the big area in Florida where very few people live. The snakes don't have any predators there, so they have become the top predator. And they get really, really big. Bigger than people. They eat people, animals, and even alligators. Someday I wonder if they'll take over the whole state and Florida will belong to the snakes."

"I am glad I am not in Florida. I do not think I would like snakes."

Something about the way he said it made her think of Dr. Seuss. The lines from *Green Eggs and Ham* ran through her mind. She kept replacing them with snakes and started to giggle hysterically.

He cracked an eye open. "What is it you find humorous?"

"I have to explain it to you some other time." She waved a hand around.

"Something from your future world?"

"Yes. Would you like to hear a story?"

She felt his forehead again. Was he warm or was it just her imagination? He looked awful. The soldiers had beaten the snot out of him. To get her mind off worrying, she told him a story from when she was little.

"I like to hear you talk. The sound of your voice makes me feel like everything will be right in the world."

It was the nicest thing anyone had ever said to her. It was raining harder and her hair was plastered to her head. She hoped she wouldn't catch a cold. The poor horses, traveling through the storm. She felt sorry for them. To take her mind off everything, she told him another story. This one true.

"When I was about five years old, I came outside the house one day. I always went through the door to the carport." She thought about how to explain it. "A carport is kind of like a stable for a car."

He made that guy sound that could mean anything. She took it to mean *keep going.*

"When I stepped outside, I saw something wriggling. I don't know what made me do it, but I jumped. It was a good thing I did. There were at least ten baby copperhead snakes on the floor. If I hadn't jumped, I would've stepped on them."

He shifted, trying to sit up. Anna pressed a hand to his chest and he stopped struggling. "Were you harmed?"

"No, but I watched them slither away, too afraid to do anything."

"I think you were very brave to jump over them."

"I didn't feel brave at the time. There was one other thing that happened when I was a child. Something I'll never forget. A couple years later, my dad took me hunting. I've always loved animals, so when we saw the deer with his beautiful antlers, I yelled *run* at the top of my lungs." She laughed, remembering how mad her dad was.

"He was so disgusted with me, he said we were going home that instant. As we walked down the dry creek bed, he grabbed me and pulled me behind him. A big black snake struck at his boot and he shot it. Before I could scream, another one came towards me. Cottonmouths are known for being aggressive. It bit his boot and he killed it as well. I was terrified. To this day I am terrified of snakes. It's one good thing about being here—there aren't any snakes."

"Is there nothing else you like about my country?"

She could feel herself blushing. "There are a few things, but I think you should rest. If you don't complain about being sick, I'll tell you when we get to the tower."

He made a face and closed his eyes. In a little while she felt his body relax. She didn't want to tell him how worried she was. He was definitely hot to the touch.

When they stopped to take a break, she called one of the men over.

"He's feverish."

The man scowled. "I care not what happens to the bandit of the wood. One of the men he killed was my brother."

Anna guessed she wouldn't be getting any help from them. She had to hope they would make it to the tower soon. Surely they would have a doctor?

Chapter Thirty-Three

As the week passed, John got sicker. Anna pleaded for the guards to help him but they refused. The general consensus seemed to be if he died along the way, oh well. They didn't care if they brought him back dead or alive.

She touched a hand to his forehead. So the guards wouldn't hear, Anna leaned close to his ear. If they knew, they would steal what little they had.

"John. Wake up. Where is your gold? I'm going to bribe the guards."

He moaned softly, blinking several times. Like he couldn't focus on her face.

"In my boots. They took what I had in the pouch. Do not give it to them. Wait until we are in the tower. Give this lot the gold and they'll slit our throats."

He was shaking, teeth chattering even though it was warm today. The nights were turning cool. It was the second week in October. Was her dad still at the facility? No. She couldn't worry about him now. John had to be the priority. If he died because they neglected him, she would beg and plead for his brothers to kill these men. She'd memorized their faces and names, hoping for payback. He was rubbing off on her. After all she'd been through, she'd started to accept the violence of the time, and wouldn't hesitate to hit back.

The next day, Anna woke to noise. They were in a long line going into the city. Some kind of toll. She laughed.

"Tolls. You can fall through time, but you can't escape them."

"A penny for the cart and six farthings for the horses, if you please."

The guards sneered. "We are on the king's business and do not pay."

The man started to protest and the guard cut him off. "If ye have a problem, take it up with the king." The man let them pass, muttering something. Anna had never been so grateful to see London.

She roused John. He was the tiniest bit better. She helped him sit up as he coughed and swayed.

"The toll is charged to help pay for street repairs. You can see the streets are full of mud and water."

Talking was a good sign. A huge wave of relief rolled

over her. While he still felt incredibly hot to her touch, maybe his fever would finally break today.

At the tower, the darkness chilled her. They half carried, half dragged John behind her. When she tried to help, one of the guards slapped her across the face.

A large man stood in front of them. His belly hung over his hose and his long tunic looked like it had never been washed.

The man looked at John and grinned, showing a mouthful of rotten and missing teeth.

"Welcome back, *Lord Blackmoor*. We missed you. It wasn't very nice for you to run off without saying goodbye."

John raised his head, bleary-eyed. "Go to hell."

The man chuckled and walked down the corridor. When you showed up as a tourist to visit the place it looked completely different than when you viewed it from the perspective of a prisoner. Anna hated to think what kind of vermin must be creeping around in the darkness of the cells.

They came to a cell she recognized. It was the same one John was in when she freed him. John saw it too.

"You kept everything ready. How kind."

"Throw him in. Put the wench in the cell next to him."

Anna pulled back. "Please. He's ill. Send for a doctor. And I am not an English citizen. I demand to be released."

"Hear that, boys? The lady demands to be released."

The guards snickered. Anna couldn't help it—she stuck her tongue out at them.

The man in charge laughed. "I am the constable of the tower. You will pay for your accommodations here or you will be cold, starve, and die."

The guards trudged down the corridor. As the man turned to go, she reached out through the bars.

"Wait."

He came back, leaning close. It took everything she had not to reel back from the foul stench of his breath.

"There is enough here to pay for our well-being. And for a doctor." The man reached for the bag, but Anna snatched it back. "I know there is also enough here to get a message to his brothers."

She stood there looking at him, knowing full well he could easily take the gold. But there seemed to be some kind of code for bribery. He picked his nose and nodded.

"I'll see it done. I will return for the message. Give me the gold."

She passed it through the opening, sending up a prayer he wouldn't simply pocket it.

"Please. He's very sick."

The man grunted and walked away.

She couldn't believe she was in jail. The sound of the door closing, the key turning in the lock...such final sounds. Anna wanted to cry.

They'd all laughed when one of the tour guides

pushed a bunch of them in and shut the door with a clang. It certainly felt different when it was for real.

John lay on the bed shivering. Anna moved as close as she could.

"John. Get under the covers."

He grunted but didn't move.

"You have to get up. Now."

He sat up with a frown. As he tried to stand, he fell to the floor. Her heart sank. He wasn't getting better like she'd hoped; he was getting worse.

He made it to the chair, sitting down with a thud, breathing heavily.

"You must write a letter to your brother. To all your brothers. I gave the constable your gold. He said it would take care of us and he would send for a doctor. I made him promise to get a letter out."

"You gave him all the gold?"

She thought she was going to cry. He braced his hands on the desk and stood. Pushing off, he stumbled over to her, taking her hands through the bars.

"I am not displeased. You did what you thought right. There is plenty of gold there. More than enough..." She didn't have to hear him say it to finish the sentence. For she knew. More than enough to pay for his burial and to take care of her and possibly pay for hers. She'd heard the guards. They said she was going to die for helping him. At this point all she could focus on was John. How sick he was. There would be plenty of time later to worry about herself.

"Can you write the messages? Do you want me to do it?"

He swayed but did not fall. As he weaved and wobbled back to the chair, he looked like a drunk.

"Nay. I will do it."

It was agonizing for her to watch him scratch out the messages. She could see the effort it cost him. By the time he was done, the sweat was pouring down his face and he was shaking. She could hear his teeth chattering across the small space.

Once more he dragged himself over to her, the messages grasped in his hand. But this time he slid down, sitting on the floor. She reached through the bars, taking the scraps of paper.

"You have to get into bed and cover up."

He shook his head and reached into the pouch at his waist. He came out with something brown. Anna looked at what he held, not sure what she was looking at. Then she gasped.

"How?"

He pressed it against his lips.

"When they cut your glorious hair, I saw the strands blowing away on the wind, I grabbed what I could. I would keep this part of you with me always." He tucked it back in the pouch.

Anna thought there was a leak in the ceiling and water was dripping on her, until her vision blurred. She was crying.

He reached through, wiping her tears away. "Do not weep, my darling. You must hear me."

She shook her head, not wanting to hear what he was going to say. Afraid.

"If I die…"

"Don't say it. The doctor's coming you'll be fine."

"You are my sun." He took her hands in his, the heat from his fever melting into her bones. "When I die, have the constable send for my brothers. They will do all in their power for you. They will aid you however they can. I—"

He was prevented from saying more as the constable came back.

"I haven't got all day. Give 'em here."

Anna passed the notes through the bars. "Is the doctor on his way?"

"He'll be here in good time."

The man left and Anna watched all their hopes go with him. She had to believe the doctor would come.

"John. Get into bed. Please. Do it for me."

He grunted and somehow got to his feet. He fell onto the bed, and she thought it would have to do for now. He had no more energy to even pull the cover over himself.

What was he about to say when they were interrupted?

Chapter Thirty-Four

Anna was exhausted, and yet knowing how sick John was, she felt guilty for sleeping through the night. She got up from the makeshift pallet on the floor and stretched, easing the ache in her lower back. Peering through the bars in the dim light, she held her breath.

Was he breathing? The moments ticked by as she looked for a sign. Over and over she grabbed handfuls of her skirts, clutching the fabric in her fists and letting go. His chest moved. She blinked to make sure she wasn't seeing things, and it moved again. Slowly up and down. He was alive. A bit shaky, she sank down on the low wooden stool.

Before she'd fallen asleep last, Anna heard John tell the guards to provide better accommodations for her. The men ignored him. They wouldn't unless they thought he was being put to death soon or was dying. Her food had gone downhill as well. No longer hot, it was now rock-filled bread, and cheese with watered-down wine. Seeing her treatment degrade gave her a sinking feeling. How much worse would it get if he were no longer here to watch over her? The sob caught in her throat. She couldn't think like this. For his sake, she had to stay positive.

A mouse darted into the cell, looking at her. She couldn't eat, so she broke off a tiny piece of bread and threw it to him. He grabbed it and scurried back through the bars.

Did they remove the bodies right away? If they didn't, the thought of mice and rats gnawing on him was enough to make her sick.

The entire day, she cajoled, pleaded, and yelled. Anything to get a response from John. Late that afternoon he started to hallucinate. Wiping her nose on her sleeve, she banged on the bars.

"Get the constable. Right away."

The guards ignored her until they probably got tired of her yelling. The constable looked like he was in a grouchy mood when he finally showed up.

"What do you want? Keep screaming and I'll have you gagged."

Her voice was hoarse and rough from screaming. "Please. Get a doctor. I'm afraid he's going to die."

The man was unmoved. "Denby said let him die."

"No. You cannot."

The man turned and walked away from her. Anna curled up in ball on the pallet, rocking back and forth.

By the time they brought supper, it was taking longer and longer for John's chest to rise and fall. And she could hear what sounded like a rattling sound as he struggled to breathe.

The guard slid her food through to her. She grasped the bars, pleading.

"I beg you. Get him a doctor." The man ignored her, and she tried one last thing. "If he has the fever, you will all get sick and die."

She was happy to see the man looked nervous. He scurried down the corridor. She wished with all her might he would do something.

Anna had been so worried about John that she hadn't even tried to go home. Once everyone was asleep for the night, she stood up. Her head ached like it was full of cotton, and her throat was scratchy. She was getting sick. Anna stood in the center of the cell and looked up to the sky.

"I want to go home. My father needs me. Please send me back." She closed her eyes and waited. Counted to twenty. When she opened them, she was still in the cell in medieval England.

All through the night she tried. No matter what she did, nothing worked. She'd searched every inch of her cell and still didn't have the locket. She didn't see it in his cell. Either one of the guards found it and took the piece, or it was where she couldn't see it. Then again, it might not be there at all. Maybe it was still in her own time. If it was necessary for her to go home, she was stuck. Unable to help either of the men in her life.

Through John's small window she could see the dawn breaking across the sky. She had to accept she was trapped in the past. And she also had to accept she might be alone. Might die in the tower.

Footsteps sounded down the corridor. Anna was too emotionally exhausted to move. She sat on the pallet and stared through the bars at John.

A man appeared. By his dress, he could only be someone important. He wore velvet and silk, and the colors were so bright in the dimness they made her head ache.

The man sneered at her. "Is he dead yet?"

"Who are you?"

The man straightened up. He looked like a peacock. "I am Lord Denby and your fate is in my hands."

"Why don't you come closer?"

He was afraid. Worried he would get sick. But the pig

leered at her. He made her skin crawl.

"Guards."

Hope flooded her veins. Was he going to do the right thing and take John to a doctor? Her hopes were dashed as they opened the door not to his cell but to hers.

"Bring her. I would have speech with her."

Somehow the sound of his voice had done what Anna could not. It roused John from his stupor. He staggered to his feet, fell, and crawled across the cell.

"Leave her be. I will see you in hell, Denby."

The man scoffed at him. "You'll be dead soon and you'll be waiting a very long time for me, Thornton."

Chapter Thirty-Five

As the guards dragged her down the corridor, Anna screamed and kicked. But after their treatment on the journey to the tower and three days in a cell, she was growing weaker by the day. And she was getting sick. She hoped they all caught whatever it was and died.

Why were they moving her to another cell? The door opened and she found herself pushed into a room unlike anything she had seen so far. The chamber was richly appointed with plush carpets on the floor, tapestries on the wall, and a roaring fire in the hearth. And there was nice furniture and no mice waiting for crumbs. At least that she could see. Anna groaned in pleasure as she stood in front of the fire, warming herself.

"Much better than where you were, yes?"

She turned to see the man responsible for her

current circumstances.

"I'd like to go back to my cell now, please."

He curled his lip. "You will bathe and eat a proper meal."

Lord Denby opened the door, calling into the hall, "Come. Help her bathe and dress. Wash what she is wearing."

He pointed to a platter on the table. "Eat. Drink. When I return, we will have speech together."

Anna had no idea what he was up to, but she needed to keep her strength up. When the opportunity arose, she would try to escape. Get help for John. He was so weak that she knew he was dying. Hope was all she had left. Hope the messages were sent to his brothers and soon they would show up. Hope was the only thing keeping her going.

"Eat, mistress. When the bath is ready, we will let you know."

She sat down at the table and inhaled the hot food. Was it good? Anna didn't know. All she knew was she was hungry, and down it went. There was even a cloth napkin to wipe her mouth. As she sipped at the wine, she noticed something glinting under papers on the table.

Sliding the papers to the side, she stared, unbelieving. The locket. She looked around the room to see if anyone was there. One of the women was busy heating water and wasn't paying any attention. She slid the locket over and looked at it.

It looked new. But it had been almost three months since she'd seen the original, so she couldn't be sure it was the same one. The locket was empty. Where was the portrait? The front of the piece was missing the indent she remembered. Maybe it had gotten banged up over the years? After all, it'd been almost seven hundred years. She ran her finger across the surface and turned the locket over. She frowned.

Still. It didn't hurt to try. Anna grasped it tight in her palm and closed her eyes, whispering, "Take me home. I want to go where I am needed."

"Mistress? Your bath is ready."

It hadn't worked. She dropped the locket, guiltily sliding it back under the papers. Anna stood still as they undressed her and helped her into the tub. The water was blissfully hot and there was a sliver of some type of lavender-scented soap. She started to wash herself but the women took over. It was an odd sensation to have someone else bathe you. Scrubbing every part of you. *Every* part.

When they washed her hair, scrubbing her scalp, she almost fell asleep. Though it felt odd not to feel a long coil of hair down her back, the heaviness when her hair was wet. Now it was light. She wasn't used to short hair. The women helped her out of the tub, and she stood in front of the fire as they rubbed her dry with soft cloths.

The women were quick and efficient as they dressed

her. The dress was a pretty green, though it had a bit of an odor to it. She sniffed. It wasn't too bad. As they sat her down and combed her hair, one of the women clucked her tongue.

"Who did this to you, mistress?"

She couldn't look at the woman. The kindness in her voice was enough to make her start crying. Instead she bit the inside of her cheek, afraid that Denby was somewhere nearby, listening. No way did she want to sound weak.

"The guards did it when I was captured."

"Bunch of brutes."

The other woman nodded. "Heard the bandit killed six of them. Good for him."

Anna sat on the stool staring into the fire as the women finished cleaning up, coming and going. She paid them little attention, too busy trying to recall exactly what the original locket looked like. It definitely had something on the front, where this one did not. And the inscription. It said, *All our years together*.

Could that be right? She couldn't be sure, since the inscription on the other one was worn off but...after she and Charlotte talked, Anna was convinced the locket had been meant for her. If it was supposed to be hers, what did the words mean? Was it that she had been here many years before the locket was given to her? Or was it a different locket?

She was growing drowsy sitting by the fire when the

door opened.

"Praying for an outlaw?"

She opened her eyes and stood up.

"John will die a traitor's death or of his illness, it matters not. The king listens to me. I am an important man. My sire wanted to behead him and be done with it, but I argued for having him drawn and quartered and hanged, as a bandit should be."

He walked over to her. The fire crackled, making her jump. She moved three steps back. There was something about him that made her uneasy. The look on his face made her wish to be invisible.

"I will let you watch from this room when your lover is killed."

"You're disgusting."

Denby grabbed hold of her face in his palms and tilted it to the light.

"What does he see in you? You are so plain. My Letitia was known across the kingdom for her beauty. You are too ugly for one as important and rich as me to bed. Mayhap I'll have you scrub my floors. The bandit's woman on her hands and knees in my home. I would like that very much."

Yuck. What a creep. The thought of him putting his hands on her was enough to make her gag. The man sauntered over to the desk and rooted through the papers. Anna held her breath. He came back with the locket in his hand and a small bundle wrapped in cloth.

"This arrived today. Word travels fast around London. The jeweler sent it here."

He handed her the locket.

"I paid for it, as I was curious to see what trinket he wanted you to have. But this..."

He handed her the bundle. It was light in her hands. She unwrapped it and gasped. Goosebumps broke out all over her skin. She bit her cheek hard until she tasted blood. When he turned his head, she stuck her finger in her mouth and touched the blood to the locket. Anna held both items in her hands, closed her eyes, and wished. She was still wishing when she heard his voice. She opened her eyes to see she was still in the past. Her shoulders slumped.

"The bastard never gave my beautiful Letitia jewelry." He made a face. "You are plain and require adornment."

She looked at the locket again. There was something different about it. But it had to be the same locket. There was no way there could be two. So she was truly trapped in the past. Her father would never know what happened to her. It was a small thing to be happy he had Alzheimer's, for at least he wouldn't miss her. But she was so worried about where he would end up without the money to help pay for his care.

And she still had to deal with the fact she was in the past and sentenced to die. Had she traveled through time just to end up dead?

Something wet landed on the portrait of John. He looked so handsome. It was snatched out of her hand.

"Give it back. He would want me to have it."

Denby sneered at her and ripped the portrait in half. It gratified her to see it was difficult for him to rip the canvas. Then he threw the pieces in the fire.

The man tossed the locket to her. "You can keep the trinket."

She snatched it and held it close.

"Guards."

Anna looked down to see only one piece landed in the fire. She dropped to the floor, reaching out, snatching the other half. Before he noticed, she jammed it in the locket and snapped it closed. It was the half she had seen in her own time. This was the locket she had found in the future. Which meant she couldn't get home. She was trapped here for as long as she might have left.

Chapter Thirty-Six

The guards took Anna back to her cell. As they opened the door and pushed her in, she automatically looked to John. The bed was empty.

"Wait."

One of the guards turned.

"Where is he?"

"Lord Denby had the bandit taken to see the physician."

"But he hates John."

The man heaved a long-suffering sigh. "I know not what goes through the minds of nobles."

The hours passed excruciatingly slowly. As evening turned to night, she could hear prisoners moaning as they fell asleep. Hear the guards laughing and talking to each other. It was full dark and still he had not returned.

She stayed awake as long as she could.

"I demand to see John Thornton."

Robert Thornton stood, hands on hips, arguing with the guard. Exasperated, he held out a bag of coins.

"For your troubles?"

The guard licked his lips, reached out, and snatched his hand back.

"I cannot. Lord Denby threatened to kill us if we allow you to see the bandit or his woman."

"Bloody hell. Denby has gone too far." Robert stomped away from the guard and went back to his carriage. At the tavern where the Thornton brothers had taken lodging, he strode through the doors and kicked at the table.

"I take it you did not see him," Edward said.

"Denby has forbidden the guards to let us see John or Anna."

"Denby has lost his wits. 'Tis time for us to take action." Christian paced back and forth across the floor.

"Edward. You should go home," Robert said.

"The hell I will. I will not leave John to die."

Robert watched as Henry leaned forward, putting his

hand on Edward's shoulder. His brother always had the ability to calm Edward before he went into a rage.

"Robert is right. You should stand apart. The king may no longer favor you if we press forward."

"Damnation. John is my brother. I will not let him die because some arrogant whoreson is jealous over a wife he cared nothing about. Letitia is dead. He parades his new wife before the king to offer her as mistress. He cares not for women."

Christian grinned. "With all of us together, the king will have to agree."

"Aye," Henry said. "William and James will stand with us. Whatever is needed. Gold, men. They will aid us."

Edward stood up, placing his palms flat on the table. He looked around the room and spoke in a low voice, full of controlled anger.

"We will offer enough gold and men that the king will not refuse. When the war is over, we will likely suffer for daring to push him into a corner. I care not. I lost John once, will not lose him again. Will you stand with me, brothers?"

Robert spoke first: "I will stand."

"As will I," said Henry.

"'Tis only gold. Easy enough to come by. I don't have as many men as the rest of you, but I will send all that I can. I will stand with you, brothers." Christian slammed a fist on the table.

"So be it," Edward said. "I will seek an audience with the king today."

Robert sat in the chair, tipping it back. "We will get John back. Denby will die for his treachery. And later, if the king goes against us, let his men come."

All morning long, Anna paced back and forth, frantic with worry over John. After lunch, which they all called dinner, she was trying to come up with plans to escape when she heard a commotion.

The guards were coming. She peered into the gloom. They were dragging someone. The door to his cell opened and they tossed John on the bed. His face was battered and bruised. Blood spattered his tunic.

"What did you do to him? He's sick. You're going to kill him."

"He was tended to by the physician." It was the guard who had been the least mean to her that spoke. Two of the guards chuckled as they turned their backs and left.

Anna leaned against the bars staring at John.

"What happened?"

"Denby and I had a difference of opinion," he rasped out.

"I hate that wretched man."

John rolled to his side with a grunt and opened an eye. The other one was swollen shut. In the light coming in from the window in his cell, his normally golden skin looked gray.

"You were alone with Denby. Did he harm you in any way?"

She waved a hand. "I'm fine."

"Tell me."

"He gave me this." She pulled the locket from her pallet and held it through the bars. John tried to get up but fell back on the bed. He managed to lean up on his elbow, and squinted toward the object.

"A locket?"

"He said you were going to give it to me."

"Nay. That is not the locket I had made for you. The jeweler making the piece was to mount a large emerald on the front. To match your eyes. Denby stole it, or someone else did." He coughed and coughed, the rattling sound making Anna go cold all over.

He reached for a cup on the table and took a long drink.

"I had a portrait made for you."

Tears filled her eyes. "I know. He showed it to me and then he ripped it in half and threw it in the fire. I was able to grab the bottom half." She opened the locket, reaching out as far as she could to show him.

"Did you like it?"

"Of course. You are the most handsome man I've ever laid eyes on."

"More so than my brothers? Christian will be wounded."

"I haven't seen Christian yet. But I know you are the most handsome of all your brothers."

He feebly reached in his pouch, pulling out her lock of hair, rubbing it back and forth between his fingers.

"I would keep you with me always. I thought to have your portrait made for me. To carry with your lock of hair."

She wiped the tears away, sniffling. "I would like that very much. What is supposed to go on the other side of my locket next to your portrait?"

He was silent for so long that she was afraid he had lost consciousness. She'd started to call for the guards when she heard his voice. More of a whisper.

"Have you tried? Can you go back?"

"No. I cannot. I've tried and tried."

"I am sorry, my love. I know how much you worry over your sire. And I feel like a bastard for being happy to have you with me. Before we were captured, I had hoped you would do me the honor of becoming my wife.

"I would have a portrait of our children painted for the other side of your locket. But you would be the wife of an outlaw and a traitor to the crown. The wife of a fallen lord with no title. I had no right to ask one so full of goodness as you."

"I don't care about your title. I don't care about any of it. I care about you. The man."

"If we weren't here, awaiting our deaths, would you marry me, Anna Waters?"

"Yes. I would marry you." Anna had put aside romance novels after her mother died. She thought there was no more room in her life for romance. But it seemed there was room; she just had to fall through time to find it. If she had been sent back because John was the man for her then why would the powers that be take them away from each other?

"I love you, John Thornton. No matter how much time we have left."

He didn't speak.

"John?"

She saw the rise and fall of his chest and exhaled a grateful breath that he had fallen asleep.

"If there's anyone up there listening, please don't let him die."

Chapter Thirty-Seven

For the first time since she was imprisoned, the guards came and led Anna out of the tower.

"Where we going?"

"Lord Denby says you may walk in the garden."

Something fishy was going on. But she was grateful to be out in the sun and see the sky for the first time in a week, so she didn't complain. They took her to the garden adjoining one of the towers. There was a chill in the air but she didn't care. Anna slipped off her shoes, feeling the grass between her toes. She touched the flowers and the leaves, tilting her face to the sun.

Maybe this was a good sign. Could John's brothers be inside securing their release? As much as she had been inside over the past years, she was grateful for any chance to go outside. Whenever she got a break at work,

Anna would slip out to enjoy the sun and the breeze on her skin.

In a much better mood, she followed the guards back inside and down the corridors to her cell. Wait. His cell was empty again.

"Has John been taken back to the physician? I thought he looked a little bit better when I woke."

Instead of answering, they pushed her in the cell and locked the door without meeting her eyes. Her heart started to beat erratically.

"Where is he? Please. Tell me."

Fear reached up and wrapped itself around her heart and throat, making it hard to breathe.

"Did you enjoy your time in the garden?"

Anna whirled around to see Lord Denby.

"Is John with the physician again? Surely that's good."

"You do not know?"

His voice sounded funny. As if it were muffled.

"Let me be the first to tell you. John is dead."

She blinked, turning the words over and over in her mind. No, that couldn't be right. He must've meant something else.

"No. He's sick but he seemed better this morn."

"It is a good day. The bandit of the wood is dead."

Little black spots danced before her eyes and the sound of wind filled her ears. Then there was nothing.

Anna woke to find herself on the floor. Had she fainted? Her head felt like it was full of cotton.

"What a horrible dream." She turned to tell John about the awful nightmare and saw the empty cell. But it wasn't a nightmare. It was true. He was gone.

She pulled her knees to her chest, rocking back and forth. Horrible noises came from deep within her chest, the sounds more animal than human.

One of the guards shouted at her, "Hush, wench."

Anna lifted her head. "Please send for his brothers. They must know."

The guard shook his head. "There is naught I can do."

Anna screamed and cried until her voice gave out. Unseeing, she rocked back and forth, the grief penetrating every cell of her body. Somehow, she'd had the ridiculous thought she would be prepared if it came to this. If he didn't get better. When her mother died, Anna thought she'd never smile again, but losing John...

If it was possible, his death ripped her insides apart. Just when she'd come to accept her love for him, to know he loved her in return...he was stolen away. How could life be so incredibly cruel?

Dinner came and went. She refused to move or eat. Didn't feel the cold seeping through the stone or hear anything. No, she was focused inward. Remembering every look on his face. Every word he'd spoken to her. How could he be gone? No one was as full of life as he.

"Dry your eyes, wench. I'm to take you to Lord Denby."

Anna no longer cared what they did with her. The guards had to pick her up and carry her. Her legs wouldn't support her.

"She's here, my lord."

The door opened and she found herself in the same room as before.

"I will not be disturbed."

The guards left, shutting the door behind them.

"Why do you cry? He is not worth your tears. Do you think he cried when my Letitia died? No, he did not. And he would not cry for you."

She looked up to see two of him. Blinked several times, and the two compressed into one hideous man.

"My family will be the greatest family in history to serve my sire. Edward Thornton squandered his chance. I made sure of it. I knew Letitia would cause trouble over John to the king. That the embarrassment would make him cast the Thorntons out of favor. So I bided my time and made sure the new king would have need of me." He shrugged and drank his wine. She watched the red liquid dribble from the corner of his mouth, down his chin, and onto his tunic.

"'Tis the way of the world."

He handed her a cup. She sat in the chair looking at it, the words washing over her, not making sense.

"There is something about you which pleases me. John took from me and I will take from him. Your ugliness will not matter in the dark. I will have you. And when I tire of you I will have you drowned in the Thames."

"You will never have me. I despise you."

He grabbed her by the arms, making her cry out. "I will laugh as they drown you."

She struggled and tried to pull away, but he held tight. Anna kicked out at him and he backhanded her so hard she fell to the floor, seeing spots. The taste of copper filled her mouth.

She shook her head, trying to clear it. And then he was pushing her down, his knees between her legs, fumbling at his waist.

She cried out, "No. Do not do this."

The door banged open and suddenly he was no longer on top of her. Anna scrambled to her feet, pulling her skirts down.

Robert Thornton stood over Denby, who cowered on the floor. Anna looked behind him to see a man so richly dressed he could only be the king.

The king took in the situation and scowled. "We have heard more than enough. You have much to answer for, Denby."

Chapter Thirty-Eight

Denby got to his feet bowing and scraping.

Robert leaned down, offering his hand. "Are you unharmed?"

She got to her feet and made a very clumsy curtsy. "I'm well. You got here just in time. Thank you."

She looked at the king. He was dressed in sumptuous black velvet and cut a striking figure. Right now he looked extremely angry, and she hoped she wouldn't be on the receiving end of that anger.

"Lord Denby, you are hereby banished from court. You may keep your title and your smallest estate. The rest of your holdings and your gold belong to us."

Denby sputtered, but before he could utter a word, the king raised a hand.

"Be grateful we let you live. You lied to us, betrayed

the Thorntons all because of your pride. Let this be a lesson to you. Now begone from our sight."

She'd never really gotten the big deal about royalty in the present day. But seeing him in this room, how he commanded the space, she understood.

The king either ignored Robert or forgot he was there. He gazed at Anna, a strange look on his face.

"We had a dream. In it I swore to aid a girl I found in the forest. She looked like you. I will grant you one request."

If only he could've come sooner. Anna's throat closed up, and she had to clear it twice before she could speak.

"Lord Denby betrayed John Thornton for his own ends. Will you pardon him?" She knew he was gone, but it mattered a great deal to her, and she knew he would be pleased his name had been cleared, even if it was after his death.

The king frowned. "We grant your request. But we do not wish to ever see him at court." He turned to Robert. "Do not think I do not know what you and your brothers were up to. Plot like this again and not only will I take everything from you, but you will all die. Painful deaths."

Robert inclined his head. "Yes, sire."

Anna could see the tiny smile playing at the corner of his mouth.

"Come, Robert. We would have speech with you." Robert leaned close and hugged her. "I will have a carriage waiting to take you to the tavern where my brothers are."

She wanted to stop him. Wanted to ask where they were burying John. And why he didn't seem more upset? But he hurried behind the king, and she guessed when you were commanded, you obeyed.

They left her in the room and she didn't know what to do with herself. When no one came, she walked toward the door.

One of the women who had helped her bathe came running toward her.

"Follow me, mistress. I am to take you out of the tower."

Anna followed behind the woman, unable to believe she was free. And how bittersweet her freedom was, knowing she had lost the only man she'd ever loved.

"Lord Thornton left this cloak for you."

"Thank you." Anna wrapped it around her and pulled the hood up over her head. It was drizzling. She didn't know what she had expected. Not trumpets or fanfare, but something to mark her release. Was this what it was like when someone was released from prison? Did they walk out the gates with no fanfare, all alone, and feel some type of letdown?

The drizzle turned to rain, which quickly turned to a thunderstorm. Her hand burned and she looked down to see she was grasping the locket. Thunder boomed and lightning lit up the sky.

There had been a storm when she had tried to go back. Could it be that simple?

The garden was close, so she stopped there. She held out the locket, let her hood fall back, and called out, "Send me home. I'm ready to go."

When nothing happened, she remembered the blood. Maybe it wasn't enough before. As much as she hated to do it, she broke the locket in half at the hinges. The jagged edge would work. She pushed her sleeve up, took the metal, and slashed her arm. The pain left her breathless and sent her to her knees. As she watched the blood drip onto the grass, Anna tilted her head up to the sky as the storm raged around her.

She screamed as loud as she could, "I want to go home."

Thunder sounded so close to her she felt the ground rumble. Dizzy, she looked down. There seem to be an awful lot of blood. Blackness descended.

Anna came to, slowly opening her eyes. It was still raining and everything looked the same. But was it the same? She sat up, wincing, as her arm throbbed.

The smell was the first thing that told her she was

still in the past. And she saw a guard walk by. It was time to let go.

Anna opened her hand to see the locket. The side with the half portrait of John. The other half lay in the mud.

"I'm sorry, Dad." Anna hoped they would declare her dead quickly. She had a tiny life insurance policy. It wouldn't mean much, but she thought it might cover the fees at the memory care facility for the next year or two.

She got to her feet, swaying, dizzy from the blood loss.

"Mistress. Why are you standing in the rain?"

It was a man she had seen out in the corridor. He was with the king earlier.

"I have nothing more to live for. He's gone."

The man looked confused. "Who is gone, lady?"

"John. John Thornton."

The man's face brightened.

"Nay, lady. He is not dead. He was ordered moved by my sire. The Thorntons are a good ally to have. They convinced the king of the truth."

Her heart leapt in her chest. "Why didn't the king tell me?"

The man clicked his tongue. "There is a war on. The king cannot be bothered with such details. I tell you, John Thornton is alive." He took her arm. "And pardoned, thanks to you."

"Is he really alive?" She was afraid to believe. Afraid

of her heart breaking all over again.

But the look on the man's face told her it was true.

"Alive, and the fever has broken. He will live." The man frowned. "Though he is in an ill humor."

She felt her entire body fill with light. "I have to go to him."

"He is waiting outside the gates in the carriage, lady. Go to him. The king has given his blessing for you both."

Anna ran.

"Wait, mistress." The man came after her. "This way."

She saw the carriage. And a man leaning against it.

"John!"

His head snapped up and he limped toward her. Anna threw herself into his arms. "I thought you were dead."

"I thought I was too. Robert told me what happened. Are you sure you are unharmed?"

"I'm better now."

"Don't cry, my love."

She looked up at him. "They're tears of joy."

He helped her into the carriage. "Christian said Denby was found an hour ago drowned in the Thames."

"Did you?"

"Nay. I do not know how it happened. Some said ruffians robbed him; others saw an old woman."

"Good."

He chuckled. Then he pulled her onto his lap,

holding her close.

"Did you mean what you said?"

She leaned her head against his chest, hearing his heartbeat. She could tell he wasn't fully recovered, but he was on the mend and everything would be fine.

"What I said?"

"Will you make me the happiest man in all of England and be my wife?"

"Yes." She threw her arms around his neck, pressing her lips to his. He tasted of brandy, his cheek scratchy from stubble, and she felt intensely alive for the first time, maybe in forever.

Chapter Thirty-Nine

They spent the night at the tavern. Anna was overwhelmed with all his brothers together in one place.

A few days later, they were in the carriage approaching a castle.

"Which brother lives here?"

"Christian. The White Castle is his."

"It's very beautiful."

John wanted to swear. Blackmoor wasn't fit for the pigs to sleep in, let alone his lady. He had much work to do.

The carriage came to a stop and he helped her out. They were in the courtyard when the jeweler rushed over. The dark clouds opened up and it started to rain. They all huddled in the stables.

"My apologies, my lord. The wrong locket was

delivered to you."

Anna reached in her cloak.

"It got broken." She held out the pieces of the locket.

John clasped her hand around it.

"Never mind. I will pay for it." He took the locket from the jeweler, holding it up. Even in the waning light, he could see how beautiful it was. The emerald a clear green to match her eyes.

The jeweler had taken the broken piece from Anna and was looking it over. He took the torn portrait out. John dropped the locket into his hand and watched as the jeweler fit the portrait into the locket.

The man handed it to Anna along with the broken piece.

"Sir, your carriage is ready."

"I must return to London."

John closed the door on the carriage and thumped it to tell the driver to go. He turned to Anna and saw her holding up both pieces. As she closed her hand around the broken piece, she winced.

He could see where the edge had cut her finger. As he watched, three drops of blood landed on the emerald of the locket.

She cried out as lightning filled the stables.

Everything happened in slow motion. In one moment, Anna was standing in the stables with John, staring at the locket. The real locket she had found in the future. Though this one had the emerald. And when she blinked, she was no longer in the stables.

She heard his voice calling to her from a great distance, but as she turned her head she found herself in a beautiful garden. Flowers everywhere. And a woman sitting on a bench.

Anna made her way to the woman and let out a cry.

"Mom."

Her mother turned and opened her arms. Anna threw herself into them.

Her mother stroked her hair. "Don't cry, my darling child."

Anna sat back and looked up at her mother. She looked as she did before the cancer. "I don't understand. Where are we? Am I dreaming?"

Her mom looked a little sad.

"I can't stay long. But there's someone else who wants to see you."

Anna looked up to see her dad. He looked like a younger version of himself, before he had been struck down by the stroke and Alzheimer's. He hugged her so tightly she squeaked.

Her mom wiped her eyes. "Thank you for taking care

of him."

"I like the short 'do." Her dad kissed the top of her head. "I know I didn't always know you, darling daughter. But don't ever doubt I didn't love you."

"We both love you. We always will. But it's time to go."

Anna didn't want to leave. She wanted to stay with her parents. Talk to them.

"Dad, I've been so worried about you. That I couldn't be there to keep paying the fees on the facility. Are you... did you die?"

He stroked her hair. "Death is the next fork in the road. Don't worry about me, honey. Live. Wring every second of joy out of life. Be happy."

She turned to her mom, who said, "You fought for what you believed in. For the man you love. Now go back to him, honey. Don't worry about your father. We're together now."

She didn't want to go, but she knew she must. With tears streaming down her face, Anna hugged them both one last time, willing her hug to say everything she could not. As she turned around, she saw storm clouds in the distance.

"Walk through them, honey." Her mom smiled. "He's waiting for you."

Anna opened her eyes to see beautiful brown eyes with flecks of gold looking down at her. She wrapped her arms around him. Anna was where she belonged. At peace.

"Don't ever give me such a fright again," John said. "You faded before my eyes. I could see through you, and yet you weren't gone."

He couldn't say everything he desired without breaking down and bawling like a babe.

"Did you go back to your future world?"

"Not exactly. I found myself in a beautiful garden. My mother and father were there."

She looked at him, and he could see the love in her eyes. John thought she'd never looked more beautiful.

"They told me everything was all right." A tear slid down her face. He reached out with a thumb to wipe it away. "I know my dad died. He wouldn't have been there with my mom otherwise."

She sniffled and didn't protest when he carried her into Christian's hall. John shook his head at the servants and carried her up the stairs. He found the first chamber and kicked the door shut behind him. He gently placed her on the bed, lying next to her.

"My parents told me they were fine. Not to worry and to live life." She looked up at him, a glorious smile on her face. "They said to live life as if every day were our last. And I plan to do so."

"Would you like to be married here? Christian's home is in much better repair than Blackmoor."

"No. Take me home to Blackmoor. I want to be married there. Surely by now the roof has been repaired."

"As you wish, my Lady Blackmoor."

"I've never had much money. I don't care about money or titles. And I have nothing to offer you. You know I can't cook or sew or anything else."

"'Tis a good thing I'm rich again. We will have servants to do all those things. You, my lady, your only duty is to be by my side. Forever."

"That I can do."

Books by Cynthia Luhrs

Listed in the correct reading order

THRILLERS
There Was A Little Girl
When She Was Good - January 10th, 2017

TIME TRAVEL SERIES
A Knight to Remember
Knight Moves
Lonely is the Knight
Merriweather Sisters Medieval Time Travel Romance
Boxed Set Books 1-3
Darkest Knight
Forever Knight
First Knight
Thornton Brothers Medieval Time Travel Romance
Boxed Set Books 1-3
Last Knight

COMING 2017 - 2018
Beyond Time
Falling Through Time
Lost in Time

My One and Only Knight
A Moonlit Knight
A Knight in Tarnished Armor

THE SHADOW WALKER GHOST SERIES
Lost in Shadow
Desired by Shadow
Iced in Shadow
Reborn in Shadow
Born in Shadow
Embraced by Shadow
The Shadow Walkers Books 1-3
The Shadow Walkers Books 4-6
Entire Shadow Walkers Boxed Set Books 1-6

A JIG THE PIG ADVENTURE
(Children's Picture Books)
Beware the Woods
I am NOT a Chicken!

August 2016 – December 2017 My Favorite Things
Journal & Coloring Book for Book Lovers

Want More?

Thank you for reading my book. Reviews help other readers find books. I welcome all reviews, whether positive or negative and love to hear from my readers. To find out when there's a new book release, please visit my website http://cluhrs.com/ and sign up for my newsletter. Please like my page on Facebook. http://www.facebook.com/cynthialuhrsauthor
Without you dear readers, none of this would be possible.

P.S. Prefer another form of social media? You'll find links to all my social media sites on my website.

Thank you!

About the Author

Cynthia Luhrs writes time travel because she hasn't found a way (yet) to transport herself to medieval England where she's certain a knight in slightly tarnished armor is waiting for her arrival. She traveled a great deal and now resides in the colonies with three tiger cats who like to disrupt her writing by sitting on the keyboard. She is overly fond of shoes, sloths, and tea.

Also by Cynthia: There Was a Little Girl and the Shadow Walker Ghost Series.